WHEN SAKURA FALLS

PART 2 OF

TALES OF ETERNAL SOULMATES

By

Liona Karman

Dedication

"To Love of My Life, Scotty,

who loved me more than any man ever could

and had to leave early for me to fulfill my true purpose in life.

Rest in peace until we meet again, My Love."

Acknowledgment

To all broken-hearted lovers in the world who have lost their soulmates and search for the meaning of their cruel fates.

To all scholars and scientists who research the power of the human soul as a formidable bioenergy that lives beyond our physical time and space.

And to the brilliant scholars at the University of Virginia-Division of Perceptual Studies, including the founder, Dr. Ian Stevenson, who diligently and bravely carries on the scientific study of extraordinary human experiences and capacities.

Table of Contents

Prologue

The heavens stretched endlessly, a canvas painted in hues of gold and silver, where time flowed like the gentle murmur of a celestial river. Soft petals of light drifted through the sky, shimmering with the warmth of a love that once was, a love that had endured beyond the limits of mortal life.

Lydia stood at the edge of eternity, her form radiant yet weightless, her heart full and aching. She gazed past the veil separating the heavens from the transient world below. There, in the dim glow of candlelight, lay King Edward, her beloved—his once-mighty frame now frail with age, his silvered hair a testament to years of battles fought and kingdoms ruled. His breath was steady and peaceful, as though even death had bowed in reverence to his noble soul.

Tears glistened in Lydia's eyes as she whispered, "My King…."

A gentle wind stirred, carrying a soft, melodic, eternal voice. "Do not weep, Child of Light," came the soothing tones of an angel standing beside her. Clothed in robes woven from the stars, the angel's presence exuded a serenity that touched Lydia's soul. "Love such as yours is never lost. It is merely reborn."

Below, King Edward exhaled one final breath, his lips curling into a soft smile as if sensing her presence. The room around him flickered, dissolving into the golden light of dawn. His soul freed from his body, wrapped in peace, vanishing into the embrace of eternity.

Lydia closed her eyes, pressing a trembling hand to her heart. "Must this be the end?"

The angel stepped forward, lifting a hand towards the boundless sky. "No. Love endures. Love returns. And so shall you."

A burst of light enveloped her, the heavens swirling like a flowing river. Visions danced before her eyes—cherry blossoms falling like snow, the clang of steel upon steel, the whisper of a name carried on the wind… Yuki.

The hush of twilight wrapped around him like a silken shroud. King Edward lay upon his grand bed, though the weight of gold and velvet now felt no different from the dust of the earth. The fire in the hearth burned low, its embers flickering like memories of life slipping through his fingers.

His body had weakened, but his soul burned with one final longing. His shallow yet steady breath carried a name that had never faded, never lost its power.

"Lydia…"

His failing eyes sought the shadows beyond the candlelight, and then—he saw her.

Bathed in an ethereal glow, Lydia stood before him, untouched by time, her beauty as radiant as the first day he had loved her. Her wavy hair cascaded like rivers of light; her eyes, pools of longing and devotion, gazed upon him with an ache that spanned lifetimes.

"I have waited for you, my love," she whispered, her voice a breeze in the dying night.

A tear escaped the corner of his aged eyes. His heart swelled, yet a cruel force pulled her image further away, like mist slipping through his fingers.

No… not again.

He reached for her, but the abyss widened. He knew this pain. He had lived this pain. They had been torn apart once before—not by time or fate, but by envy and dark magic.

His mind drifted to the past, to the moments that had led to their tragic seperation…

Once, in a life adorned with crowns and duty, King Edward had been a king, and Lydia his queen. Theirs was a love whispered in secret chambers, sealed with stolen kisses, fierce and unbreakable.

But love that shines too brightly is often the target of darkness.

Matilda—once Lydia's trusted sister—had longed to be the king's queen, her heart twisted with unfulfilled desires. But it was not love that burned in her—it was obsession, hatred, and hunger for power.

And she was not alone in her malice.

Cassandra, the witch who dwelled in the cursed forests beyond the kingdom's reach, had long coveted Lydia's soul. She had seen a light in her, a radiance untouched by corruption. And for a heart as black as Cassandra's, such purity was threatening and unbearable.

It was Matilda who sought her out.

"If I cannot have him," Matilda seethed, "no one shall."

Cassandra granted Matilda's wish, her dark lips curling in cruel amusement. She wove a spell born of old, forgotten magic laced with shadows and venom—a curse upon eternal love.

With whispered incantations and the blood of the innocent, they bound Lydia and the king's souls, ensuring that no matter how many lives they share, their love would always be torn apart.

Always just within reach. It's always just too late.

And so the curse was carried out.

Lydia had fallen first, drowned by the twisted cruelty of Maddox, King Edward's half-brother who stole the crown. The King was lost in a battle and then his amnesia, orchestrated by Maddox and his evil Queen Mother, till it was too late. His kingdom crumbled beneath war, betrayal, and ruin. He recovered his crown with the help of Lydia's soul and angels, and now, his death came like a lover's embrace, cruel yet inevitable.

Their love, meant to last an eternity and to bring light to the world, had instead been cast into an endless cycle of loss.

The past faded like mist in the morning sun, and King Edward was once again in his dimly lit chamber, his breath slowing, his heart whispering its final beats.

But he was no longer afraid.

He had seen the truth. He had seen her.

Even if a thousand lifetimes stood between them, even if they were to be born into different lands, different times… he would find her.

He forced his trembling lips into a smile.

"Lydia…" he whispered again, his voice stronger this time. "No curse… no god… no fate will keep me from you. I vow it. Wherever you are, I will find you. I will always find you."

A breeze stirred through the chamber—not the wind of the mortal world, but something else. A force unseen, a whisper of destiny shifting.

And then—his eyes closed.

The world faded.

But far beyond the veil of life and death, beneath a sky where cherry blossoms fell like whispers of forgotten vows, a young orphan boy named Hajiro awoke from a dream of a woman he had never met… yet loved with all his heart beyond reason.

Chapter 1

Under the Sakura Tree

Feudal Japan, 1540

The sky stretched pale and endless over the village of Chita, streaked with the first blush of dawn. A boy of nine, wrapped in tattered cloth, stirred from his restless sleep. Hajiro blinked against the dim morning light filtering through the cracks of the rundown hut. His breath curled in the frigid air as he sat up, pressing a hand to his chest, where his heart pounded in a rhythm he did not understand.

The dream again.

Invariably, the dream.

A place he had never seen, a castle not of wood but stone, towering beneath an unfamiliar sky. The air smelled different there, crisp and foreign. And within its walls, she stood—a noble lady, her robes flowing like rivers of silk, her voice whispering to him through the fabric of time itself.

Her presence felt like home, but her face remained a mystery. But, somehow, his heart knew he was destined to love her, for eternity.

"Who are you?" Hajiro wanted to ask.

But as always, the dream dissolved before he could reach her. A cruel trick played by the heavens.

A sharp voice shattered his thoughts.

"Lazy boy! Get up before the merchants take everything!"

Hajiro saw the village elder's wife scowling at him from the doorway. Her skin was as cracked as the rice fields in summer; her mouth twisted in permanent displeasure. He knew what would come next.

A sharp slap against the back of his head. A reminder that he was no one.

Hajiro ducked his head and muttered an apology, slipping into his worn sandals. He stepped outside, greeted by the scent of damp earth, wood smoke, and rotting fish from the market stalls.

The village of Chita was dying.

The wars between the daimyos had drained the land of its strength. Ronins, once honorable Samurais, now roamed as bandits. Farmers who had once toiled in golden fields now carried swords, fighting battles that were not theirs. And orphans like Hajiro? They were nothing but ghosts, drifting through a world without a place for them.

"But I am more than this," Hajiro told himself, fists clenched.

His father had been a warrior, a samurai who once served a noble lord. But a masterless samurai was a dead man walking. His father fought and fell when war came, leaving Hajiro with nothing but a name too insignificant to be remembered. His mother died young, giving birth to Hajiro.

Hajiro ran through the village streets, his feet bare against the dirt. He weaved through merchants setting up stalls, past beggars fighting over spoiled rice, past the women who whispered pity when they saw his thin frame.

"I am not weak," he wanted to scream.

But strength meant nothing when his stomach gnawed at itself.

Hajiro's daily task was simple—steal or starve.

He approached a rice vendor, the scent of warm grains stirring hunger so sharp it was painful. His fingers twitched. The merchant turned, and Hajiro moved swiftly, snatching a handful of rice from a sack before bolting.

"Thief!"

The merchant's cry split the air, and Hajiro ran.

Through winding streets, broken alleyways, past children who looked just like him—hungry, hollow-eyed, and waiting for something more.

But there was nothing more.

A strong hand caught his arm, yanking him backward. He hit the ground hard, dust stinging his eyes. The village elder loomed over him, disappointment heavy in his gaze.

"A Ronin's son, reduced to stealing scraps?" The old man spat. "Your father would weep in his grave."

Hajiro gritted his teeth, his nails digging into his palms. He did not cry.

Not when they took his father's sword.

Not when he had to beg for rice.

Not even when he dreamed of a woman whose name he did not know but whose soul called to him across the ages.

That night, as Hajiro lay on the cold dirt floor of the hut, hunger clawing at his ribs, he let himself remember.

The castle of stone. The lady was draped in a crimson velvet gown. The voice he could not hear but felt deep in his souls.

"Who are you?" he asked the darkness.

There was no answer.

But deep in his chest, something stirred.

A feeling beyond hunger, beyond pain.

A knowing.

He was meant for something greater.

Even if the heavens had abandoned him and fate laughed in his face, he would find her. Someday. No matter how long it might take.

The Sakura Festival, 1540

The scent of Sakura blossoms drifted through the air, carried by the gentle spring breeze. The poverty-driven village of Chita was unrecognizable today, adorned with banners of crimson and gold lanterns swaying like fireflies beneath the endless sky. Laughter and music filled the streets as merchants called out their wares, and children ran barefoot, their voices chiming with delight.

Among them, a small girl, no older than seven, wandered away from the procession. Draped in a silk kimono of the finest lavender, her obi tied with intricate patterns of cranes and flowing rivers, she looked like a vision—a tiny goddess who had stepped out of a painting on a Byobu screen.

The golden crest of the Matsunaga clan shimmered on her sleeve, a silent declaration of her bloodline. But Yuki was lost in the wonder of it all. Her father, the powerful Daimyo Matsunaga Hirotada, had brought her to witness the Sakura Festival for the first time. Yet, she had wandered too far.

She turned, but the sea of unfamiliar faces blurred together. The guards who had stood so rigidly beside her moments ago were gone. Panic swelled in her tiny chest.

Then—

A deep bellow. A beast's cry.

The ground trembled beneath her feet. An ox, massive and enraged, barreled through the street, its tether frayed, its eyes wild with fear. It plowed through a vendor's stall, sending crates of rice and pottery flying. The villagers screamed, scattering like fallen leaves.

Yuki stood frozen beneath the towering Sakura tree, its petals drifting lazily, oblivious to the chaos below. The ox's massive horns gleamed under the afternoon sun; its rampage directed straight at her.

And then—

A blur of motion. A boy leaped between her and the beast.

"Run!"

Yuki gasped as Hajiro, dressed in tattered rags, lunged forward. His tiny hands grasped the discarded banner of a merchant stall, whipping it up with the instincts of a survivor. The ox snorted, hooves pounding into the earth just inches away. Hajiro's heart slammed against his ribs, but he did not falter.

He waved the banner wildly, the fabric snapping like thunder. The ox, startled by the sudden flash of color, reared back, its momentum broken. At that moment, Hajiro seized Yuki's wrist and pulled her away, sending them both tumbling onto the dirt road.

Dust settled. The ox was subdued and caught by its handler. The world around them blurred back into reality.

But Yuki was only aware of one thing.

The boy who had saved her. His hands were rough, his clothes torn, his hair unkempt—but his fierce eyes held a warrior's unwavering resolve.

"Are you hurt?" Hajiro asked, breathless.

Yuki blinked, then shook her head, still dazed. "No… you saved me."

Before Hajiro could respond, the heavy pounding of boots surrounded them.

"Yuki-sama!"

The Daimyo's guards appeared, blades half-drawn, their eyes wild with terror and fury. And behind them, Matsunaga Hirotada stood, his presence towering over all. His face, usually impassive as stone, was twisted with barely restrained panic.

Yuki scrambled to her feet. "Otosan!"

She ran to him, clutching his sleeve. The Daimyo knelt before his only child, his calloused hands cradling her face, searching for wounds that did not exist.

"I am unhurt, Father," she whispered. "This boy saved me."

The Daimyo's gaze lifted, settling upon Hajiro. Silence fell like a blade.

Hajiro lowered his head. He knew his place. A peasant should never meet the eyes of a lord.

One of the guards stepped forward, hand on the hilt of his sword. "Oyakata-sama, he is a vagrant. Shall I remove him?"

Yuki's tiny fingers clenched into her father's sleeve. "No!" She turned to the Daimyo, her voice firm despite her size. "He saved me."

Lord Matsunaga studied the boy for a long moment. There was something about him—a fire in his gaze, an instinct beyond his years.

"You are Ronin-born," the Daimyo said finally.

Hajiro stiffened. Even now, the ghost of his father's honor haunted him.

"Yes, my lord."

The Daimyo's expression was unreadable. Then, he rose, his voice carrying the weight of command.

"This boy shall be Yuki's playmate and bodyguard."

The guards gasped. Hajiro's head snapped up. Had he heard correctly?

Yuki grinned, clapping her hands in delight. "Father?"

The Lord nodded. His heart warmed at Yuki's smile, who lost her mother at a young age and has been lonely in a guarded castle without any siblings to play with.

"A debt must be repaid. And a samurai's path is not chosen by birth alone." His gaze fell upon Hajiro once more. "Do you accept this duty?"

Hajiro's breath caught in his throat. His hands curled into fists.

A chance. A path forward. A life beyond scraps and stolen meals.

He bowed deeply, forehead touching the ground. "I will protect Yuki-sama with my life."

And so, his training began.

Days passed, and the bond between Hajiro and Yuki deepened.

What began as duty became a friendship. What started as protection became devotion.

Hajiro trained under the Daimyo's finest swordsmen every morning, his body hardening with each strike, fall, and lesson in discipline and honor. By dusk, he was Yuki's companion—her shadow, sword, and closest friend.

Yuki, mischievous and stubborn, tested the patience of every retainer in her father's court. But Hajiro never failed to find her when she strayed, to stand between her and danger, to hold her secrets as if they were his own.

And with each passing season, his heart betrayed him.

His heart grew to love her.

Not as a hime, a princess, he served. Not as a friend. But as a girl who he wished to be his.

Yet—he was only Hajiro, the orphaned son of a fallen samurai.

And she was Yuki-sama, the daughter of a daimyo, a princess. A woman promised a future far beyond his reach.

Still, under the Sakura tree where he once saved her, Hajiro silently vowed.

"Even if I can never have her, I will stay by her side until my last breath."

Fate, however, had other plans for both.

Chapter 2
The Ancient Curse

The moon's silver glow spilled across the hidden cave where shadows danced on the rippling waters of a secret pond. Kurojin stood deep in this darkened sanctuary: the most feared Onmyodo sorcerer of his time, shrouded beneath a midnight robe with sigils of forgotten spells, staring into the shifting surface of the water. At the same time, his shadowed eyes narrowed in preparation for a vision.

It was not just any pond, but the portal, the bridge to other worlds, and the sacred mirror of time. Kurojin traced his fingers to the air, and then the image sharpened. There stood Hajiro and Yuki, two soulmates united together once again by destiny, under the blooming Sakura tree. Kurojin's expression twisted with a flicker of rage. He knew these souls. He knew them long ago through a poisonous, revenge-filled, unfulfilled soul called Matilda.

Past, called memory from a world long buried in time, resurfaced in his mind. He closed his eyes as his spirit ascended beyond this mortality barrier and surrendered to the pond's dark magical lure. Suddenly, the waters deepened like a swirling abyss, and the cave dissolved around him.

Kurojin opened his eyes to meet the grand corridors of a medieval castle in the Kingdom of Zuzu. Grand stained-glass windows let in an array of kaleidoscopic hues across the marble floors while a faint echo of solemn chanting resounded in the sacred halls. A long time ago, this was his home when he walked these halls as Cassandra, the infamously powerful witch of the kings and queens.

Clouded memories swept through his mind like blades. Hatred, betrayal, desperate hunger for power – these caused Cassandra to unleash her curse upon King Edward and Lydia, binding their souls in the cycle of tragedy that would last for ten lifetimes. The dark forces had granted Kurojin a chance for another life to finish the curse Cassandra had begun.

Muffled footsteps echoed on the old, ancient altar. Leftover relics of age were still eagerly waiting in the air, and tapping in a conspiratorial whisper, the shadows twined and twisted and summoned the specter of Cassandra. The translucent form of her draped in spectral silk smirked at him.

"You have come back," she said, as a shred of a past melody. Kurojin bent his head slightly as a tribute to the witch who once was a form that contained his soul, "It's time now to finish what had begun. They will not escape again."

Cassandra's evil laughter filled the chamber. "Then let's make sure you do more than curse them. Break them for eternity."

****

Long shadows of a lone monk strolling along the winding dirt streets of a village, devastated by war, could be seen as the sun was hiding away from the world. His ragged, dust-caked, dark clothes did nothing to hide his unusual aura.

Kurojin had wandered thus far in search of one soul to execute the will of the past. And there, he found her amongst the ruined spaces of what were once homes.

A child hardly past her seventh year squatted by the charred remains of what used to be a shrine, clutching a broken fox mask in her tiny hands. Tangled, unkempt strands of hair flecked with dirt cascaded over her hollow eyes, which seemed devoid of tears. She had long run out of them.

"You are alone, My Child," Kurojin said, low but firm.

The girl did not flinch. She looked up at him with an unsettling steadiness for one so young. "Alone is all I have ever known."

Kurojin's contemplation flickered for an instant in those darkened eyes. This child! Not just an orphan of war. She was Matilda reborn. The remnants of her old soul were felt restlessly awaiting an awakening.

"You dream, Little One, don't you?" he mused, kneeling before her.

She hesitated. "Of a castle," she whispered. "Of a woman with curly raven hair and a voice like fire. She speaks to me in words I do not know, yet I understand them." Then, her fingers tightened on the mask. "She tells me I have been wronged."

Kurojin smiled. "She is right, My Child. And I will make it right for you. Do you trust me?"

So, from that day onward, Keiko followed the monk into the wilderness without a question nor looking back.

The Training of a Fox Witch

In an ancient sylvan wilderness, Kurojin began his work. He did not hug one; did not bring solace, but taught by agony, endurance, and awakening the slumbering ability within her.

"Feel the shape of your soul," he instructed.

Keiko closed her eyes and inhaled deeply, filling her lungs with moss and burning incense smell. In her mind, she envisaged herself, seeing not a child, adding something else. Something liquid. Something untamed.

"The fox is your true form," Kurojin said. "A creature of deception. Of trickery. Of magic."

The first time she changed, it was agonizing. Her bones twisted, and her skin burned, but when she opened her eyes again, she stood on four slender legs, her fur a shimmering silver beneath the moonlight.

"Good," said Kurojin, satisfaction and fatherly pride lacing his voice.

Every day, he saw the growth of her shadowy strength. She learned the art of illusion, bending shadows to her bidding. Whispers wove into the wind, deceiving men and leading them into darkness. And in her dreams, Matilda's voice grew louder, feeding her hatred and hunger for vengeance.

Keiko knelt before Kurojin, her foxlike eyes gleaming with strange intelligence. She had grown; no longer the frail orphan holding a broken mask, she has become a container of the past itself in the very veins.

The shadow of Kurojin stood before her, elongated in the firelight. His voice rang out firm and absolute, breaking the silence.

"It is time."

Keiko did not ask what he meant. She knew. She had always known. The dreams of a cascading raven-haired woman whispering of vengeance, lessons carved into her body through pain and fire—everything had led to this moment. She was ready.

She got up. "What must I do, master?"

Kurojin's mouth twisted into a smile. "First, we will sever this land from its balance."

The Seeds of War

In a time and place such as feudal Japan, all had significantly changing loyalties, tenuous truces, and ambitions like the samurai's katana. The Akamura Clan had become disillusioned with Yuki's father. Lord Akamura Mitsunaga had long believed that Lord Matsunaga Hirotada, Yuki's father, was not worthy to lead their region. Cold steel, he was the one who eyed the Matsunaga Clan and had consistently earned his hatred.

But, Lord Akamura was not headed for recklessness; such an act would be foolhardy. Without sulking his name, he needed chaos and war to justify Matsunaga Clan's fall without damaging his honor or reputation.

That's where Kurojin comes in. Kurojin spreads whispers to fire the flames of betrayal by visiting the court of Daimyo Hoshino, the powerful warlord of the Tetsuyama Clan.

"Lord Matsunaga grows bold recently," Kurojin murmured, his voice smooth as oil.

"He conspires with the foreigners beyond the southern seas.

He seeks to bring dishonor upon the traditions of our land."

Lord Tetsuyama clenched his fists with displeasure as an honorable and respected war lord faithful to the old traditional ways, who was threatened by the new ways coming to his land like tsunami waves. "If what you say is true, it cannot be allowed."

Somewhere else, Keiko had also webbed another net of lies within the Shirakawa Clan, a rival of the Tetsuyama Clan. She painted a different picture to the old lord's ears through pillow talks as a devoted concubine who cares about her lord's safety.

"I have heard from a friend that Lord Tetsuyama plans to seize the lands of the Matsunaga and Akamura alike. If he succeeds, then your people will be at his mercy."

Lord Shirakawa frowned. "Tetsuyama will not stand for this."

"Not if he's finished off first, My Lord," whispered Keiko with a cruel brilliance in her eyes.

And thus, all pieces began to move.

Lord Akamura turned on Matsunaga Clan, Lord Tetsuyama acted in the name of tradition, and Lord Shirakawa sought to protect his clan at all costs. In the middle of all, the Matsunaga Clan, Yuki's family, stood oblivious that the storm had set on them for their entire clan's demise by the wicked sorcerer's trickery.

Hajiro, a now-grown young warrior, felt the shifting winds in the region's leading daimyos' political alliances. He saw how Yuki's father was troubled.

He stood under the Sakura tree one night and closed his fists. He said, "Something is coming. And when it does come, there will be no mercy."

He vowed to protect Yuki with his own life.

Chapter 3

Dragon's Breath

Feudal Japan in 1542:

The wooden halls of the Matsunaga estate blazed, turning the proud fortress into a smoking ruin of ash and cinders. Smoke as thick as evening mist snaked through the air, choking the scent of cherry blossoms with the reek of blood. Screams and steel clashed within that darkness. The gardens, once serene, were now the battlegrounds on which samurai in shining armor cut down their enemies, their battle cries coursing through the air toward oblivion along with the roaring flames. "Protect the Daimyo! Do not let them reach the Lord!" An Akamura warrior wrenched his sword free, plunging it into the blue and silver-clad samurai's throat and dropping him to his knees in a torrent of blood. Another Matsunaga retainer, stepping in to engage the enemy, felled him with desperate fury. The katana glinted in the firelight and back, impaled from behind with a spear.

Meanwhile, Lord Matsunaga Hirotada stood tall in the keep, with turmoil surrounding him. His once-magnificent armor was tainted with blood, and the gore-soaked sword felt heavy in his grip.

"Betrayal..." His voice thickened with bitter disdain, "Akamura Mitsunaga, you damn snake."

Surrounded by the last of his retainers, their numbers dwindling with each passing breath, he turned to the men again. "We fight to the last man. For honor. For our forefathers."

"FOR THE MATSUNAGA!"

The warriors charged into the storm of blades, roaring in unison.

A Father's Final Stand

In the fiery hours of the night, Yuki crouched beneath the shrine, her small hands tugging at the hem of her kimono. The heat was suffocating. With her face smeared in soot, she heard the sounds of the world breaking down outside.

The door burst open.

"Father!" she cried, stumbling into open arms.

Lord Matsunaga knelt before her, weary and wounded now, whose once-grand stature was anything but battle-torn. He held her face, his eyes gentle amid the tireless storm raging around them.

"Yuki," he whispered. "Live."

"But, Father—"

He silenced her with a grip of steel before standing tall, katana poised as shadows rushed through the doorway. Akamura samurai.

"Go." His voice was unrelenting.

The first enemy leaped forward.

The Lord's blade found flesh even before the warrior cried out. Another one came—he steered clear, twisting his sword into the ribs of that warrior. Blood sprayed across the tatami mats.

Invaders kept her father busy, but he was slow and deep in wounds.

And then came the fatal strike.

A spear thrust through Lord Matsunaga's back. The man staggered, spitting blood, and still turned, downing an enemy before dropping onto one knee.

His eyes found Yuki for the last time.

"Yuki. Run."

Hajiro jumped in out of nowhere and grabbed Yuki's hand. They ran as he took one blade after another for her.

A minutes later, Matsunaga castle crumbled under the fire.

****

The river swept Yuki away, a fragile body carried among the debris of her fallen clan. Yuki was barely conscious, and small hands clawed for something—someone—yet there was only that cold embrace of water. She was stained with the blood of Hajiro, who had passed his warmth to her but whose sacrifice was in vain.

The Sakai River knew no mercy, twisting through valleys and forests to the monstrous sea where fate awaited her.

Far across the ocean, outside war-torn Japan, a great vessel with white sails sped across the waters. Madame Élise Beaulieu, a wealthy French widow, stood at the bow, her rosary slipping through her fingers, murmuring prayers. She was a devoted woman, a member of the Congrégation des Xavières, a sisterhood inspired by Saint Francis Xavier, who had traversed these foreign lands to spread the word of Christ.

A cry from the sailors broke into the peaceful rhythm of the waves.

"Madame! Il y a quelque chose dans l'eau!" (Ma'am, there is something in the water.)

Madame Beaulieu lifted her veil and narrowed her eyes as she saw the small, pitched form flung about in the waves.

"Récupérez-la immédiatement!" (Recover it immediately) she cried.

A net was thrown, limbs outstretched, and Yuki was pulled on board. The child collapsed on the deck, still as a stone. Dark clumps of hair dripped down her white face, lips parted as though she had wished to say something just before drifting into oblivion.

Madame Beaulieu knelt next to this girl and pressed her palm to the bruised forehead of the girl.

"Mon Dieu... une enfant..." (My God, a child) was all she could whisper.

A doctor from the ship came rushing in to assess her, running his fingers along deep gashes and bruises.

"Elle a perdu beaucoup de sang, mais elle vit encore," (She lost a lot of blood, but she still lives.) he murmured.

A miracle.

"Do all you can; try to save her," said Madame Beulieu firmly.

They wrapped Yuki into fine pieces of cloth, laid her in a warm cabin, and prayed. Days passed, and the girl was caught in fevered dreams. She saw the flames eating her house and heard the clashing of metal and the screaming voices of people dying. Hajiro's voice called out her name—that river - the cold - the silence.

Consequently, she awoke in an unfamiliar ambiance, clapped up against too-soft silk sheets, and gasped while she jerked upwards.

"どこ...?" (Where...?)

Beside her sat a woman clad in odd, moving garments, whose eyes were soft but held a kind of intensity that bereft Yuki's understanding.

The woman spoke, but the language was strange.

"Tu es en sécurité, mon enfant." (You are safe, My Child.)

Yuki flinched and shrank back. The lady pointed at a man with a Jesuit priest amongst the crew. He kneeled next to her.

"この方はあなたを助けました," he translated. "彼女はエリザベートといいます。" (She saved you. Her name is Madame Élise Beaulieu.)

The lips of Yuki trembled. "私の家族は？" (My family?)

The priest hesitated. Madame Beaulieu did not know that language but recognized the signs of grief.

Reaching across the trembling hands of Yuki, She whispered, "Je suis désolée, mon ange," (I am sorry, my angel.) Her voice choked with emotion.

Yuki did not understand the words, but she understood that such words were valid. Her family was gone. Hajiro was gone. Nothing remained.

A sob tore itself from her throat.

Élise took her into her arms and close to her bosom, whispering soft prayers for the weeping child.

Thus, the girl once called Yuki became Marie-Yuki Beaulieu, the daughter of a woman who thought her a gift from God. But fate had not finished with this girl yet.

****

The waves were merciless.

Hajiro's body drifted broken and bleeding in the river's wild currents, blown away like a leaf in a tempest. Yuki's warm little hands had left his own; he had pushed her out of harm's way, taken the katana meant for her, and watched her disappear beneath the waves. His vision became foggy, darkening with loss, but one thought that was still clear: 'I saved her. She will live.'

The sea consumed him.

Hajiro opened his eyes and was greeted instead by a ceiling of decaying wood swaying along with the waves. A mix of sweat, salt, and unbathed bodies clouded the atmosphere. Hajiro felt the burning pain of trying to move painfully and became aware of the thick ropes binding his wrists; he was lying there with others of the most miserable state slaves.

A distant, loud voice suddenly pierced the dull murmur of half-conscious prisoners.

"Oi! The boy is awake!"

An immense man with tanned skin and a beard crouched next to him. The glint of the golden teeth flashed in the light. The faded pirate captain's coat the man wore was shabby at the edges, but the long sword at his side told Hajiro everything was anything but ordinary.

"A boy alive? Good fortune indeed," the man continued in a coarse accent. "The corpses we fish out from the sea, but you were still breathing. Is a boy strong enough to weather the storm? Hah! The gods must be favoring you."

Hajiro gritted his teeth. Even though he did not understand the words, he instinctively understood that his life wouldn't be any better than his years in poverty-driven Chita. He so wanted to spit at the man's feet, but his throat was too dry; it felt like he had eaten a handful of sand.

The captain laughed again. "You belong to us now. Get used to it."

A strike from a boot slammed into Hajiro, opening up his wound again. He felt his wounds scream, but no sound escaped his lips: A samurai does not show weakness.

He looked up at the ship- an ungodly ship patched from the wood of a dozen nations, sails blackened in wars of smoke and haze. Above on deck, a disorderly crew of men armed with blades and muskets laughed, brawled, and drank; they were the pirates from all corners of the Earth.

This would be his new prison: Out in the sea and nowhere to run.

****

Across the sea, in a grand French estate, Yuki sat by a window, staring at the cherry blossom tree in the garden: A rare tree in France that Madame Beaulieu brought from Japan to make Yuki feel at home.

She was safe. She had a new name, clothes, and life; Marie-Yuki Beaulieu, daughter of the kind widow, a miracle. But in the quiet moments, when the world fell still, she saw flames. She smelled blood. She heard Hajiro calling her name.

In the musings of her mind, she ran down long corridors formed from stone blocks, as if within a medieval castle, in strange, uncomfortable garb. A strikingly handsome man beckoned her while calling a name she didn't recognize.

And always, she woke with tears on her cheeks.

****

Hajiro, too, dreamed.

Through toil and the crack of the lash, through fetid rice poured down his throat, it was to a girl under a Sakura tree and her laughter, smiles, and calling out to him.

A castle in a land not of Japan with glittering armor, where he swore to protect his beautiful queen.

Yet every time he woke, all that remained was the cold reality of chains and salt air.

Both believed the other had perished.

But fate was not yet finished with them.

Chapter 4

Fate's Intervention

Feudal Japan in 1549: 7 years later:

The salty sea breeze of Kagoshima Bay carried with it the smell of foreign spices, and, above, diffused hardly, the sound of hymnals sung with dissimilar languages to the land. The late afternoon sun poured liquefied gold into the harbor, turning the wrinkled waters and rippling surfaces into molten silk. Hinging upon a hundred fluttering banners in the stirring winds—the fierce crests of daimyo clans, the crimson and white flags of Iberian merchants, and the most sacred emblem among them, the Society of Jesus, marked with a golden sunburst upon pure white fabric and gleaming like a divine beacon.

Hajiro stood straight, hands clasped behind him, among the throngs, waiting to watch the ships as they drew closer. He had seen many boats that any man had not seen in his lifetime. Dark pirate vessels sail like tattered ghosts; warships reeking of death; merchant junks heavy with treasure. These ships were different.

They were grand, pristine, almost ethereal in their presence. Their sails bore the mark of a mission, not conquest.

Beside him, Antonio, the man who had taken him from the horrors of captivity and shaped him into something more than a mere slave boy, whispered, "They bring the Word of God, Hajiro. But they also bring the winds of change to Japan."

Hajiro remained silent. His deep eyes, as dark as midnight oceans, scanned the human forms on the ship's deck. There were Jesuit priests who stood quietly, swaying in their black robes with the breeze—nobles and wealthy benefactors who could afford to support such a voyage- who stepped down slowly onto the docks.

Then he saw her. A vision woven together of dreams and memories waltzed out of the ship's shadow and into the sunlit pier.

At that moment, the rest of the world froze around him.

She was nothing like this land had ever known.

Her flowing cascade of sinewy gold and soft pink gown rippled with each delicate movement imparted upon her. The lace at her sleeves drifted softly in the gentle warmth of the air that bore the breath of Sakura petals in spring. About her feet, silk chopines raised her above the wooden planks, where stories in embroidery talked to her from far-flung lands. A white lace parasol, as delicate as a butterfly wing, shaded her face, protecting her translucent porcelain skin from the sting of the sun.

And her hair-well, that was a statement in its own right; Western-born charm and artistry that speak of diligent handiwork, luxuriously tied up in fancy, sweeping curls, loomed over a face with a different kind of familiar aura that had turned the air within Hajiro's lungs to stone.

His heart was beating like a hammer inside his ribcage.

It was her.

It was Yuki.

But not Yuki, whom he knew. Not the girl who had laughed under the Sakura tree, not the child whose body he had shielded with his own against katanas. This was a reborn woman clad in Western splendor with an independent grace that belonged to the noble.

None were corrupted, God, that gaze.

They were as terrifyingly unchanged.

The same quiet strength, kindness, and sorrow were there in Yuki's eyes from the day their world was charred into nothing before Hajiro-their light dimmed near extinction.

Yuki stepped onto the dock, fussing with the lace of her glove. Beside her, a priest greeted the daimyo and his men in slow, deliberate Japanese.

But Hajiro heard nothing.

All the cacophony from the harbor—the shouts of merchants, the crashing of foreign seas, the cries of fading seagulls—were gone now and lost in the overwhelming silence engulfing them.

And like time had carved years between them, like oceans had swallowed their past, and fate had clothed them in lives scarcely recognized by the other—yet her soul knew his.

A sharp breath caught in Yuki's throat, the lace parasol in her hand quivering slightly.

Frozen stood Hajiro, breathless with uncertainty, mind racing toward grasping the impossible between them. Yuki. Not a ghost. Not a wishful dream. She was there--flesh and blood, standing underneath the golden sun that had shone on many of their childhood days.

Yuki, clothed in a delicate silk of the West, clutched the lace of her glove, her eyes wide and incredulous. Could it really be? The boy who had thrown himself in between her and danger, the one who had laughed with her under the Sakura tree, the boy she thought she had lost to the river's cruel embrace-him still alive!

They did not speak to one another.

And then Yuki ran.

She was running to him, abandoning her silk chopines as they fell from her feet, arms reaching out-gaining momentum to break through the invisible barriers of time and suffering that had guarded them from meeting again. Hajiro seized her, arms tightening around her; he feared that she would vanish if released.

"You're alive," whispered Yuki with a quivering tone of disbelief.

"And you live," breathed Hajiro, resting his forehead against hers. He felt her warmth, the undeniable truth of her existence. Once hard and calloused from chains, his hands now cradled something far more precious than freedom.

They stayed in that way for a moment, a moment snatched from the hands of cruel destiny, left untouched by the ravages of war and suffering.

Time, ever merciless, dragged them back.

Hajiro stepped back, dark eyes memorizing every inch of her face. "I thought you had died that night," he finally confessed.

Yuki swallowed, nodding. "I thought the same about you." She took a deep breath before continuing softly. "Tell me, Hajiro. What happened after the river took you?"

His face shaded over with a darkness, and shadows crossed his face. "Pirates pulled me from the sea...They did not see a child. They saw a slave." His tone remained even, but Yuki heard the burden within. "For years, I was nothing but a tool to them. I scrubbed the decks, unloaded their cargo, and suffered beatings when it pleased them. I learned their language, how to bargain, how to survive."

Yuki's hands clenched at her sides. The thought of Hajiro suffering alone on an unnamed ship, under the hands of heartless pirates, ripped her heart apart.

"But you managed to escape?" she asked, her whisper barely audible.

"I was freed," Hajiro said, the weight of memory making his exhale catch. "Antonio... he found me, saw something in me. He taught me to read to speak like a scholar instead of a slave. He gave me purpose. Now I am a translator and a liaison, talking with men of power, even people like Oda Nobuhide."

Yuki gasped. "That Oda Nobuhide?'

Hajiro nodded. "Yes. Daimyo of Owari. Feared and respected by both sides."

Yuki gazed upon him, looking for the face of a boy she had once known. Even so, that boy still lived in him, carrying the burden of a life that had been thrust upon either of them.

"Hajiro," she whispered and stepped closer. "So much you've had to endure." She lifted her hand, hesitating at first, before lightly touching his scarred palm. "And yet, you've become someone extraordinary."

Hajiro chuckled softly. "Just a boy who survived."

Yuki shook her head. "No... You are so much more."

Hajiro, utterly taken with the gentleness in her tone, lifted a hand to tuck a straying curl behind her ear. "And you?" he asked. "Tell me about your life, Yuki."

A faint smile played across her lips. "I was saved," she said. "The river flowed to the sea, where Madame Beaulieu—a Frenchwoman—found me. She was a true Catholic, a woman who had always wished for a child but had never been blessed with one." Yuki's eyes softened. "She took me in, raised me like her own daughter, and gave me a life I had never thought possible."

She gazed up at him. "I was given love, safety, and education. And in return, I chose to dedicate my life to the mission of God—to serve others, as I was once saved."

Hajiro smiled faintly. "That sounds like you."

She blinked. "Like me?"

"The girl I knew was kind, compassionate, and selfless." His voice warmed, gentle. "It seems time has only knit together what was already there."

A soft laugh escaped from Yuki. "And yet we are both so different now, Hajiro."

He nodded. "Yes."

They maintained silence between them, not awkward, but rather a silent consent.

Yuki took a breath as if hesitating to ask, "Will you stay?"

Hajiro's expression grew more difficult than before. "I cannot. My duty—"

"I know," she said softly with her eyes downcast.

Hajiro hesitated again, then placed his fingers under her chin, gently tilting her face upward again. "But I will see you again."

Her lips went apart in surprise.

"At the Sakura Festival," he told her. "Where we first met." His voice had a promise about it, one as solid as the tides. "On the night when the cherry blossoms dance in the wind, I will be there."

Yuki's eyes shimmered with some unuttered thought.

"Under the same tree?" she asked.

Hajiro nodded. "Under the same tree."

She smiled as bright as the golden rays of the sun above them.

"Then I will wait for you there."

And in many embraces and caresses, two souls, torn apart by war and fate, were again being threaded into one promise of tomorrow—one written in the petals of the cherry blossoms to come.

Chapter 5

Whispers of Darkness

Deep in a haunted labyrinth, with twisting paths that no mortal would dare travel, there was a hidden cave- the domain of untouched time yet swallowed by darkness. Here, Kurojin, the sorcerer of Onmyōdō, bound with sublime incantations the very fabric of fate.

At the cave's entrance stood two stone statues, silent witnesses, forever frozen in agony. Once men, they were now mute reminders of Kurojin's cruelty- the punishment of all who had dared challenge him.

Inside, the cavern walls pulsed with ominous light, and ancient inscriptions etched into the stone glowed in a sinister flickering crimson. The air was thick with the burning incense mixed with something decay-like: the scent of sorcery past and curses yet to be unleashed.

The deep chuckle echoes through the hall.

Kurojin, dressed in dark and crimson robes, was seated on the bank of his sacred pond- a pool darker than the void. The water's surface rippled, and two figures embraced-Hajiro and Yuki-at the pier by the sea.

His dark eyes were narrowed with predator sharpness.

"Fate must have chosen this reunion for you two," he said in a hissing velvet whisper. "How foolish!"

Long, clawed fingers cut the air above the pond as the shimmering water gorgeously twisted the reflection into something grotesque-one of torment and love broken by despair.

Kurojin rose to his feet and walked towards the altar, where several ancient scrolls lay unfound, inked with the forbidden spells handed down from generation to generation of dark practitioners. Flickering candlelight cast jagged shadows upon the cave walls, and the sound of spirits trapped within the cavern filled the silence.

Deep and resonant, his voice twisted and turned like a death lullaby.

"Fire to burn, wind to scatter,

Love to break, souls to shatter.

Bound by fate, now bound by a curse,

Two hearts lost, never whole again."

A tremor ran through the cave. The mist thickened. Something was approaching.

A living black serpentine energy encircled his outstretched hands to form an inky mist, which slithered along the cavern floor like a moving beast. The curse took shape, feeding on the very malice in his heart.

Outside, the forest reacted.

The ancient trees groaned as the striations on their trunks opened; out came thick vines, twisting like monstrous tendrils in search of their next victim. The stone statues at the entrance of the cave splintered and cracked, their faces twisting in agony as though they could still remember the very pain of their last moments.

Bright dots glimmered to life in the eyes of the statues.

Far in the depths of the enchanted forest, a murder of crows launched from treetop to treetop, sharp caws ringing loud with warning as if the very balance of the world shuddered.

Kurojin hissed between his teeth, letting out a slow breath tinged with an abyssal wickedness.

"It is done."

He turned his back to the pond, where the lovers' reflections shook with the shivering weight of the curse he had cast upon them.

"You will find each other again," he spat. "But not in joy. Not in peace." He glared at them, his eyes flashing gold with cruel delight. "No, my dear soulmates... your love will suck the marrow of suffering."

And as the last candle extinguished, the cave was swallowed whole in darkness, shrouding the curse in shadows blacker than death itself.

Spring's Broken Promise

Time flowed like the transient cherry blossoms, beautiful yet fleeting, an abstraction of memory. Hajiro had grown to master the art of negotiation; his voice would deftly carry messages from the Portuguese traders to the powerful Japanese daimyos. There, at the ports of packed Nagasaki and Kagoshima, he stood by his mentor, Antonio Mota, and the ever-great Francisco Zeimoto, both of whom had taken such uncommon and wondrous merchandise from the West; leather, medicines, black pepper, and most coveted muskets.

He bowed to generals in the dark corridors of forsaken castles before whom a mere word could send thousands to their graves. The burning smell of incense mixed with the acrid smell of steel as the worn-down samurai stood waiting in ostentatious armor.

"Lord Matsuda," he said with measured tones, "Your armies will be invincible with these weapons in hand!"

The aging daimyo's eyes glinted as he lifted a musket and ran his fingers along the cold steel barrel. "And in return?"

Antonio stepped forward, his Portuguese lilt thick with the taste of coin. "A guarantee of safe passage for our ships and a fair share of your silk trade."

Hajiro stood watching with little expression, but in his heart, he mourned. Each deal he made, and every warlord he armed pushed him further from the life he had once dreamt of.

Far away, in another world but in the same land, Yuki knelt before Oda Nobuhide, speaking softly yet vehemently as she translated St. Francis Xavier's words.

"'The Lord speaks of love,'" she told the mighty warlord, dazzling in her exotic Western clothes against the austere background of the Daimyo's court. "A love beyond swords and blood. A love that will outlive any empire."

Oda Nobuhide narrowed his eyes. "And this love... does it make a man stronger or weaker?"

"Stronger," she said without hesitation. "For true strength comes from within, not from fear, not from war."

A scoff arose from the courtiers, but Nobuhide smiled at it. "A woman with fire in her spirit. You are unlike the others."

His son, Nobunaga, stepped forward from behind - an ambitious young warrior of fifteen, dark eyes so deeply curious of Yuki and something else… fascination.

He had never seen someone like her—bold, indeed, and unafraid; her beauty was an enigma carved by foreign hands. While Japanese noblewomen bowed their heads and whispered, she stood tall and spoke with commanding air around her.

That night, a shadow fell beside her as she walked alone along the moonlit corridors of the Oda castle.

"I've never met a woman who speaks to my father as you do," Nobunaga murmured as he stepped closer, his fingers barely brushing against the silk of her sleeve.

Yuki turned, breath catching at his stare's closeness and particular intensity. "I speak to all men as equals."

"And yet," he whispered, palm coming lightly on the wooden pillar beside her to cage her, "you are far from equal to anyone. You are... extraordinary."

She could feel the warmth of his vigorous body, the unspoken desires of adolescence woven between the silence. A part of her- a part of a young woman just blossoming in her- ached for warmth and touch from a man, and something more than duty, maybe love.

But she closed her eyes and stepped back. "My path is not one of flesh, Young Lord."

His lips curved into a knowing smile. "Not yet."

The Sorcerer's Deception

Beyond the mere limits of the human world, well-hidden deep within the cursed forest, Kurojin watched the unfolding story, satisfied with himself.

The spell was working.

Under the flickering of his candles, the surface of his enchanted pond began to twist and darken until it was Yuki and Nobunaga's seeds of temptation sown.

But it was not enough.

The distraction must be made of this world. A power. A destiny that shall hold her from Hajiro.

With raised hands, Kurojin whispered dark incantations, breath turning mist heavy with shadow.

In one corner of his cave, a fox lay curled, a creature of fascinating beauty, dull light shimmering from silver strands of fur.

Keiko.

At his command, the fox stirred and rose onto slender paws. Around it wavered the air, becoming thick with the intoxicating scent of Sakura petals.

The transformation began.

Where fur once lay, flesh grew. It became an enchanting young beauty from the fox's place, ivory skin crowned with midnight-dark hair, the color of the night sky, eyes gathered luminous amber flame. This was Keiko, a fox witch born of magic and malice.

"Give her to Nobuhide," Kurojin murmured as he traced his fingers over her naked flesh. His touch glided down the globes of skin usually covered with silks. His hand savored the hum of dark power beneath that supple skin. "She becomes his concubine, his whisper in the dark, his only thought."

Keiko cocked her head slightly, her lips curling into a slow smile. "And the girl?"

"Destroy her." Kurojin's voice was smooth as poison.

"Make her forget. Make her lose herself to Nobunaga, to this land. Make sure she never sees the boy again."

Keiko leaned against him, her breath ghostly cold on his skin. "And in return?"

"You shall be the queen of this nation when the time comes," he promised, brushing aside a stray lock of hair from her face.

"And the boy... will be left with nothing but ashes."

There was then a sultry, haunting laugh as Keiko turned away, naked in her new glorious shape, stepping into the darkness to change destinies.

The Forgotten Promise

In the faraway path, petals drifting off into the wind like whispers of forgotten love, the old tree stood, yearning under the cherry blossoms falling.

But the lovers never came.

The moon witnessed the shattered promise as two soulmates, entangled in duties and fate's web, moved farther apart.

In that darkness, the fox witch chuckled while a sorcerer smiled.

Chapter 6

Love Rekindled

Feudal Japan, 1551; Two Years Later

Gunpowder hung in the air with the scent of freshly tilled soil. The sun was drooping over the Owari province, casting ragged shadows across the field where Hajiro and Nobu stood, watching the newly fired arquebus lying in the dirt. Smoke poured from the barrel; the noise of the shot was still hanging in their ears.

Exhaling slowly, Nobu, seventeen, with sharp eyes that burned with ambition. On swords he had seen and on the cries of dying men in battle he had heard; this was something else for him. This was power.

"Nothing like I have ever seen," Nobu muttered, fingers itching to pick it up again. "With this kind of firearm, even a peasant could kill a samurai."

Hajiro smirked, "War is no longer a blood-oriented game, my good friend. The world has changed. And those who do not change with it... will perish."

Nobu turned to him, observing the man-turned-more-than-just-a-merchant's-apprentice: a sworn brother, teacher, and equal.

"You talk about it as a science," Nobu said with eager curiosity.

Hajiro knelt in the dust, parting the soil with the small dagger, "It is. Look at it this way: Alexander the Great conquered not through brute force but by knowing war. His soldiers were outnumbered, but he adjusted. Used formations that were unheard of. Turned the ground against his enemy!"

Nobu knelt beside him, eager, drinking in every word like a thirsty man at a spring: "Tell me more."

Hajiro smiled, "At Gaugamela, an army five times the size of his own stood up against Alexander. He let the enemy know he was weak, chasing shadows until they were worn out. Then, he struck where they were weakest, cutting across them like a blade through silk."

Gleamed the young Nobu's eyes. "Clever... deceitful, but clever."

Hajiro met his gaze. "It is not about honor. It is about victory. True rulers fight when necessary. Otherwise, they let their enemies destroy themselves."

A silence stretched between them, and those words began to sink deep into young and ambitious Nobu's mind. His fingers tightened around the musket's grip.

"Tell me about these Western weapons," Nobu said at last, lifting the firearm and feeling its weight and the promise it carried.

"They will change everything," chuckled Hajiro.

And so began the lessons. Between conflict and slaughter, between those moments of peace and drink, the two young men became more than allies- they became brothers.

Sworn Brotherhood

With sake fogging his mind and a glorious victory clinging to his spirit, Nobu banged down his cup on the wooden table late that night.

"Hajiro," he said slowly and loaded with emotion, "more than the life I owe you; you are not merely a friend; you are a brother."

Hajiro, with his usual calm demeanor and an amused expression, poured himself another cup. "That is not a small claim, young lord."

Nobu grinned. "I don't joke on such things. Loyalty is rare today, and I trust you more than my blood. Therefore, I swear here in the name of whatever gods may exist: you will rise with me when I rise. I will never forget either your wisdom or your sword. And should I ever break this vow, may the gods smite me."

The destiny proclamation was well said; it bore a heavy weight. Hajiro could feel it, the fire behind it, the unflinching determination. Setting down his cup, he looked straight at Nobu.

"Then I swear the same," he said, touching his heart. "Through the war, peace, whatever fate brings, we stand as brothers together."

They clasped each other's arms, thereby cementing their promise.

The wind howled through the trees outside, carrying their vow into the enveloping darkness.

Under the Sakura Tree

Cherry blossoms filled the air with their fragrance. The petals drifted serenely under the pale moon as soft pink snowflakes. Kagoshima's streets were alive with people's laughter during the festival, melodic flute tunes wafting through the air, and the faint sound of wooden sandals clattering against stone paths. The lanterns danced along with the flickering shadows on the multitude of ancient trunks of Sakura trees.

But for Hajiro and Yuki, the festival was a vivid blur, somewhere far away from the sacred place where they waited.

Under that same tree where fate had bound them, Hajiro waited. His kimono of black and gold, embroidered with the crest of his Portuguese patron, sparkled in the moonlight. At his belt dangled a sword, a symbol of this world he now ruled—a world of daimyos, power, and ambition.

Then, she came.

Yuki.

Her very presence felt like the first kiss of spring. Beneath the brightly lit entrance of pink blossoms, she was more beautiful than any woman Hajiro had ever seen. Soft moonlight danced on the delicate laces of her dress, a gift from her adoptive mother. Ivory-colored material glistened like a shell. A jeweled comb glittered in her raven locks- the filigree design captured the light.

Her eyes locked with his, deep, dark, and filled with something unutterable.

For one long moment, neither spoke.

Then, as if the two years separating them had never existed, she ran to him.

"Hajiro..." Yuki whispered scarcely above a breath, falling into his chest, inhaling him and the scent of sandalwood and sea salt.

He held her close, fearing that if he let go, he would genuinely lose her. "I was afraid you wouldn't come." His voice was raspy with choking time and longing in his heart.

She pulled away to look into his face, her fingers outlining the roughness of his jaw. "I waited for you every night."

Their hands found each other, fingers entwined in a way that made the outside world disappear.

A Vow

Hajiro sighed as his forehead rested against hers. "Yuki... I have so much to tell you; so much has been happening."

"Then tell me," she smiled.

He led her to the underbelly of the Sakura tree, where the grass felt soft, and petals gathered like a plushy blanket. They sat together, her head resting against his shoulder while he spoke.

"I have become more than just a translator," Hajiro began, his voice low and full of conviction. "I am a bridge- a man who stands between two worlds."

Yuki was listening attentively to every word.

"Oda Nobunaga," he resumed, "he will be a great leader someday. I have seen the fire in his eyes, the way he looks at war like a puzzle only he can solve. He believes in me, in the future I dream of."

"And what future is that?" asked Yuki, tilting her head to look at him.

Hajiro smiled, his fingers tracing her delicate jaw line. "A Japan that is unified. A Japan that is no longer torn by war." His voice softened. "A Japan where a man like me-an outcast, a slave, a foreigner-can rise."

Yuki felt her heartache, knowing the struggles he had endured, knowing he bore the burden without anyone to share it with. She held his hand firmly. "You are not an outcast, Hajiro. Not to me."

The night was getting deep leaving the moonlit streets of Chita deserted. Between heavy breaths, the two shared silence, the only sound being the whisper of the breeze across the blossoms.

Then, Hajiro's hand found her chin, lifting her face towards his. "Yuki… I love you."

Yuki's breath caught.

"I have loved you since the first moment I saw you," he whispered. "And every day apart from you has only made that love stronger."

Yuki's eyes glistened with tears. "Oh, Hajiro..."

But, before she finished, his lips found hers hungrily, his eyes holding an incandescent fire glaring into her deepest soul. "Marry me," he proclaimed. "Next year, when St. Francis and his entourage leave for China, marry me, and stand by my side in the new world we will build together." A glimmer of joyful tears began to form in her eyes, the kind that made his heart ache with deep love.

"Yes," she breathed, her voice trembling. "Yes, Hajiro. I shall be yours, now and forever."

Hajiro's hands trembled as they caressed Yuki's face, his fingers stroking her heated cheeks. The years had been hard on them, parting them, but the gods would not rob him of her tonight. His lips crashed over hers, kissing her hotly-with desperation-for all those years of restraint, all of that pain from separation. His arms wrapped around her, pulling her against him, her body fitting against his as his hands roved over the soft silk of her dress.

She gasped as he pushed her body against the rutted bark of the Sakura tree; he tangled his fingers in her hair, tilting her head back to offer an unbroken view of her neck. His kisses, hot and insistent, then seared a descending trail along her throat, kissing, nibbling, tasting as if he wanted to claim every inch of her, to make her his forever.

Yuki shivered as her fingers raked at his robes, pushing them off his shoulders and exposing his stiff and rugged muscles. Her hands traveled across his chest, tracing the scars etched into his skin, reminders of his battles, reminders of sacrifices he had made.

"These scars," she whispered, kissing each one, "are proof of your strength, Hajiro. Proof that you came back to me." An agonized groan escaped him, and her touch caused his body to tighten.

Within one swift motion, he grasped her and brought her into his arms, wherein her legs were wrapped around his waist as he trekked further into the grove blanketed by the cherry blossoms like a bed arranged for lovers. The silver-soft moonlight bathed the two lovers in an embrace, illuminating raw hunger in Hajiro's eyes as he tenderly gazed down at Yuki. He untied the silk ribbons of Yuki's dress with his rough, urgent, but trembling hands, and pushed the fabric aside, revealing soft, glowing skin underneath. She gasped sharply as the night air kissed her bare flesh, but not before Hajiro's body swallowed hers, soaking her in his warmth like fire. His mouth found hers again. This time, it was slow, deep, savoring, and claiming. Yuki arched against him, pressing her softness to his hardness, her fingers tangling in his hair as she moaned against his lips.

His hands, now unrestrained, traced every curve of her body, memorizing, branding, until she trembled beneath him, pleading, aching, burning.

"Yuki..." His voice was hoarse, rough, and ragged breath as he buried his face against her neck. "I need you."

Her palm is cupping in his face, gazing out through her dark eyes, filled with love and longing. "I am all yours, Hajiro. I always have been and will be."

He did it with a heavy groan.

The world around them fell apart- no war, no duty, no time, only the heat of their bodies, the wild rhythm of their love, and the sound of their breaths and gasps interspersed with the rustling of cherry blossoms in the wind.

They burnt together under the Sakura tree, the entwined fates of their souls like threads on an unbreakable destiny, while the night enveloped them in eternal embrace.

As dawn came close, and the first rosy hue painted the sky, Hajiro kept Yuki close, kissing the dampness on her skin, muttering a silent vow-that there would be no more waiting, no more separation, that from that night on, they belonged to each other.

Chapter 7

The Curse Resurfaces

The air was weighed down with the night, the scent of pine and earth damp with rain coiling around the Oda estate. A soft haze encircled the stone lanterns spreading along garden pathways, their flickering flame casting the longest, sultry shadows. Somewhere beyond the walls, a lone shamisen weeps a little melody into the wind; a tune touched with sky seems to transpire through the night woods, and the stars transform it into a lover's lament.

Keiko stood, arms folded, in a pond, knee-deep in moonlit water, her bare torso gleaming under the full eruption of the pale moon. Long black hair, as dark as a raven, cascaded down her back, dancing silver droplets in the dim light above. She made the surface of the water ripple with her touches on the skin, purifying herself from the foul odor of Nobuhide.

'Disgusting old man,' she vented.

Night after night, he would come for what he wanted, turning her into little more than a plaything to help him relieve his never-ending lust. But Keiko was no such thing. She was a fox in human skin; her soul was alive and burning with ambition. She might have given him her body, yet her heart, loyalty, and dreams belonged to no man other than herself.

Tonight, she would set a new course for her destiny.

She heard the boy before she saw the reeds rustling and the quiet shuffle of footsteps on the stone path. A smirk curved her lips as she dipped her naked body lower, the water licking against her collarbones as she feigned innocence.

Nobunaga.

The young and hot-blooded heir. The one she had watched from the shadows, waiting for her moment to strike.

Returning from the drinking party at a Geisha house, his robe smelled with sake, sandalwood and perfumes, the smell of another woman still fresh. But that didn't matter.

'He'd be mine tonight.'

Keiko laughed playfully against the echo of splashes in the silence of the night, pretending she was not aware of Nobu's approach, her voice an innocent yet seductive purr against the crispy night air.

His drunken gaze halted as it cut through the mist in search of the source of the strange incantation. A flicker entered his eyes at the sight coming through the half-submerged pond, half-revealed bare skin, bright like eager flames in a fireplace.

Hunger. Keiko tilted her head as water dripped from her wet locks, staring at him with a pretend shock under her seductive lashes.

"Lord Nobunaga! You're out late. I didn't know," She pretended to be desperately searching for a cover for her exposed moonlit flesh, dripping water.

The muscles in Nobunaga's jaw tensed; his expression remained inscrutable. "Keiko? What are you doing in the pond at this hour?"

She laughed softly, "I needed cleansing."

She let her fingers glide through the water, then look to that motion. "Sometimes, a woman has to wash her filth off to be able to sleep."

This was also reflected in the clenching of young Nobu's fists at his sides. Everybody knew that his father kept young Keiko at his will, and the young warlord had always regarded her, about his age, with a certain amount of pity and disgust. He never saw her as a woman in her own right but always as his father's plaything.

But tonight. .... she saw how his gaze darkened, and his throat bobbed as he swallowed.

Keiko took a slow step forward, the water parting around her thighs as she emerged from the pond, droplets trailing down her skin in silver rivulets.

"My lord….." Her voice was soft, teasing, as she neared him. "Are you going to keep looking, or will you give me some cover?"

He exhaled sharply, shamelessly staring. "You are too young and stunning to be my father's woman."

"Another old man. Time is not on his side." She raised a slender hand and trailed a leisurely finger down his chest, tracking the beating of his heart beyond the thin fabric of his robe.

"Isn't it a pity... to waste such beauty on a man who will be dead soon?" Nobu shuddered under her touch as his bottoms got tightened. His pride wrestled against his desire, his honorable personality contending with the fire rousing in his veins.

"Dangerous games are best played alone, Keiko," he said in a low voice.

She smiled, raising her chin to lightly brush her lips over his jaw. "All good games are dangerous."

And then she kissed him as her hands traveled down to the teenage boy's hardened bottom, ready to explode.

It was a slow and tantalizing kiss, like an invitation for sin; her lips scarcely brushed against his, withdrawing slightly. A test. A challenge.

It was too much for young Nobu.

With a low growl, he seized her waist and crushed her body against him, his lips devouring hers in a kiss that left her moaning as he drank from her, claiming her mouth while allowing his hands to range freely over every inch of her wet, bare skin.

Picking her up, he emerged from the water, her legs encircling his waist as he shoved her back against a smooth cherry tree trunk.

Everything around him vanished; there was no father, no wars, no ambitions—only the fever of their bodies clashing with urgency—mouths and hands. His robe had slipped from his shoulders, her wet skin glided against his warmth, and calm breaths mingled in the intoxicating night air.

Keiko gasped when he bit down on her shoulder hard enough to leave a mark—his claim.

"Tell me this isn't some trick," he growled hotly into her ear.

She cradled his face, looking directly into his fiery eyes. "This is fate. From the first moment I stepped into this castle, I saw nobody but you. My heart beats only for you."

And he believed her.

The night was a magnificent symphony of moans and groans, with whispered names and tangled limbs. Their bodies moved in a fevered dance of panicked passion and strength.

Keiko arched against him, feeling him everywhere, filling her and shredding her inside in the most delicious way. Young, strong, unyielding was the antipode of his father.

This was power. This was everything she wanted.

As morning light painted the sky with crimson and gold, Keiko lay beside him on the soft bed of fallen petals, drawing lazy circles on his bare chest.

Leaning in, her lips brushed his ear. "Promise me something when your father dies."

Nobu stiffened slightly. "What?"

She smiled and pressed a lingering kiss to his jaw. "Make me yours."

His arm tightened around her, his fingers tangling in her hair as he pulled her closer again. "You already are."

But deep down, they both knew the truth.

Keiko was no man's woman.

She was a woman of no one but herself.

And with young and ambitious Nobu in her clutches, the dangerous game of power within her had only begun.

The Ashes of a Dynasty

The funeral pyre was set ablaze and burning high toward the midday sky, curling thick black smoke into the heavens, almost as if calling upon the spirits of the ancestors. The scent of burning wood and incense mixed with something more bitter: something final, that of death. And so the monks chanted slow and rhythmically in unison, their voices, the haunting lament of the soul for the great Daimyo Oda Nobuhide, who had ruled with an iron fist and was feared by enemies as well as revered by the vassals beneath him.

Now, he was but ashes waiting to be scattered.

The Oda retainers stood in solemn rows, bowed heads, and clasped hands before them in respect. The family, draped in serious-looking white and black robes, watched the flames consume the once mighty lord in the hum of Buddhist monks' chants.

But one man did not bow. One man did not weep.

His second son, Nobunaga.

The young heir stood away from the others, currently crimson-stained in fluttering robes blowing to the wind with his sword tied loosely at his hips. He had not shaved his head in mourning or dressed in white as the custom. Instead, he regarded his father's burning corpse with a smirk that sent a ripple of unease through the lords and vassals gathered.

"Tch." Nobu clicked his tongue and tilted his head, looking at the fire dance.

He stepped forward, each footfall adding weight to the heavy silence of the mourners. It was now deafening with the crackling of the pyre, and a thick, humid air sealed his lips, but he did not falter. Nobu, always the unruly son, never the obedient heir, stood before his father's body and scoffed.

"This ends it, Father?" he murmured mockingly. "Burns like some common peasant. What happened to the great warlord, the indomitable daimyo?" He chuckled, shaking his head. "How pathetic!"

The crowd gasped. To insult the dead, and especially one's father, was known to be the worst thing imaginable in the land of Japan.

"Nobunaga-sama, please..". A tense Shibata Katsue, one of his retainers, stepped forward to speak. "This is not the time," he said.

Nobu turned his piercing gaze upon him. "Not the time?" He laughed, the sound sharp, edged with something almost mad. "Tell me, Katsue... was it ever the time for my father to treat me as less than a man? Less than a leader? Was it ever the time for him to cast me aside in preference of my weak elder brother?"

The retainers changed meaningless glances among themselves, but nobody dared to speak.

Nobu turned again toward the fire, his face bathed in golden light.

Keiko watched this from one shadowed corner, satisfied smiles curling her lips.

She had designed excellence here.

She first fed into Nobu's ears while they tangled in nights of silk and sweat, awakened his resentment, and stoked the embers of ambition.

The rare poison, born from onmyodo magic, was prepared by her and dropped into Nobuhide's tea each night until his once-strong body became frail, and then many of his warriors would whisper about some strange sickness that even the gods could not help treat. She now watched her young lover, her partner-in-crime, take his very first footsteps toward the destiny he created.

Dead was the old daimyo. A young heir now stood before the pyre as a new daimyo of Oda Clan.

A Pact in the Dark

Nobu managed to find Keiko that night after the last of the mourners had left the pyre smoking in the wind. Keiko was seated before a low candle, and the light flickered against her naked skin. She had taken off the mourning robes required by tradition and instead was wearing a crimson silk kimono more loosely around her bare waist; her long dark hair streamed down her back like a flowing river. He stood in the doorway, watching her silently, mesmerized.

"You should be in mourning," she finally said, gazing at him. "Or does the new daimyo feel nothing for the loss of his father?"

Smirking, Nobu stepped inside the room, closing the door behind him. "You're the reason I have nothing to mourn."

She arched a delicate eyebrow playfully. "Am I?"

He walked toward her with slow deliberation, like a predator approaching prey.

"You were right, Keiko," he breathed, kneeling before her. "The old fool, clinging to his power, blind to my potential. He would have let my brother have it all, that weakling." His fingers trailed over the curve of her shoulder. "But now..."

She caught his wrist, forcing his palm against her bare breast, letting him feel the warmth and the fluttering of her pulse beneath his fingertips.

"Now you're the Daimyo," she whispered, leaning in, pressing her lips to his jaw. "And I belong to you."

He sucked in a breath. "You always planned for this, didn't you?"

She smiled against the skin of his neck. "Would it matter if I had?"

His grip on her tightened as he pulled her closer, their lips crashing together in a flurry of teeth and warmth and wild hunger.

She surrendered to him, just as she had surrendered to his father. Men were means for her to get what she wanted. Nothing more. Nothing less.

He pinned her underneath him, her weight pressed into the tatami mat while he tore through the silken fabric of her kimono. Her nails raked down his back as he claimed her, their bodies colliding with an intensity that left them both breathless but burning, aching: She arched beneath him, whispering words of devotion, of power, of ambition, until his resolve melted into her hands.

"Nobu," she moaned, her lips tracing the shell of his ear.

"Promise me something." His breath was ragged as he drove into her, his body worshipping hers in the way only a man hungry for power could.

"Anything," he growled. She smirked against his neck.

"Keep me by your side. Always." He kissed her fiercely, biting her lower lip as his fingers tangled in her hair.

"You are mine, Keiko." His voice was rough, possessive.

"Forever." She closed her eyes, savoring her victory.

She had secured not only his love but his power, future, and empire in his arms. The boy she had seduced had become a warlord. And she, the woman who had shaped him, would stand beside him, hidden in the shadows, wielding the power of a queen. Forever.

The Seduction of a Warlord

Casting off her silken robes in the moonlit garden, Keiko stands, revealing flawless skin underneath. The air was thick with the scent of blossoms, concealing the darkness flourishing in her heart with its beautiful and gentle fragrances. This is the fragrance of cherry blossoms.

Her eyes are golden-hued—freakish and hypnotic—glistening like molten gold but slightly shifting as her inherent nature flickers beneath her guise of humanity. A fox. A witch. A seductress.

Men do not serve her.

Men would serve her.

Oda Nobunaga, the young, mighty warlord, is included in that.

There he comes, tall and propelling himself forward like one who knows he rules so many—yet this night, he swayed in her buttons. "Keiko," lured from Nobu's throat, his voice low and dense with desire.

She turned, slow and deliberate, as her lips formed a smile. "My Lord," she whispered, advancing a little closer, the folds of her robe brushing against him.

But he missed the self-reach because instead, she drew a single, delicate finger down his chest, making the touch as cold as ice but searing into his soul.

Her magic, old and unseen, coiled around him like invisible chains.

"Oh, you love me," she purred as she whispered the love spell in Nobu's ears, tilting her head as the light caught the faint outline of fox ears before they disappeared into shadow.

An instant of glazing took place across Nobu's eyes; for a flicker, there existed hesitation before he answered with a voice of utter conviction somehow hollow within as if something was wanting.

"Of course, Keiko, till my last breath"

And she had that smile.

It was working; her spell.

The Witch's Trap

The only other man to whom Nobu had ever laid such trust was Hajiro. Their brotherhood had been forged under conditions of blood and war, but there could be rust on the strongest steels—especially after having come into contact with a cunning fox's venom.

How easy was the scheme for Keiko?

A damsel in distress, a hero, misunderstanding!

One moonlit night, Keiko broke into weeping when the lanterns dripped low and the sake waxed generous with good cheer upon Nobu's most trusted men.

She fled from the room, her locks in disarray, her robe torn at the shoulder, a study in desolation.

Nobu was the first to see her.

His eyes hardened. "Who did this?"

She trembled her lips; her fingers curled against her chest as if trying to hold herself together. "Hajiro."

The name fell like a curse from the lips of the wind.

The men gasped.

Nobu's hands turned into fists.

"He—he tried to touch me. I refused him, but…" She looked down, letting tears fall like fragile glass beads. "He was drinking. I was afraid."

The room turned on Hajiro in an instant.

"A disgrace!"

"Betrayal of trust!"

"How dare he lay hands upon Lord Nobunaga's consort?"

Hajiro staggered forward, disbelief crashing over him like an avalanche of ice water.

"Nobu," he pressed, closing the distance toward his friend. "You know me. You know I would never touch what is yours."

Nobunaga raised a hand in disbelief. "Enough."

Hajiro froze.

His sworn brother's confused expression was no longer one of trust.

Standing just behind Nobu, Keiko slightly turned and was careful to keep her sleeve up to cover that smile.

Whispers of Dishonor

No one could describe Yuki as possessing any of Keiko's qualities, not that softness, purity, or innocence could easily be attributes associated with the opposite. She was Nobu's first crush, the one whom he admired like an angel, a saint until the venoms of Keiko crept into his life.

That itself was enough to seal Yuki's doom.

Keiko was poison and had spread her word like slow poison, forging her words like a master tactician.

There was the first rumor, a whispered folly from the hall.

"Yuki has been sneaking out at night."

Rumors glimmered high in the court.

"I saw her sneaking out from the castle at night. She says prayers, but..."

All that was left now was an accusation that couldn't be ignored.

On one such night, the moon shining withdrew into the clouds when Nobu found Yuki before the shrine, kneeling in prayer. He had watched her from the dark, his heart ready in a storm of suspicion.

And then Keiko had walked in a cool breeze against his rage.

"So you doubt her innocence, my lord?" she had barely kissed the ear with her lips.

Nobu had clenched his jaw. "I need a proof."

Keiko smiled: "Then, I shall give it to you."

Yuki was framed on the very next night.

Keiko had staged everything. The guards burst into the scene that Keiko had so carefully contrived with a hired actor.

Yuki, with eyes just soaking in everything and the pulse in her throat starting to race.

The man grins and straightens out his robe.

A single candle lighting the "truth."

The court broke into whispers. Yuki's honor was lost.

Nobu, towering above everyone else, peered down upon Yuki, his eyes confused and icy.

She neither pleaded nor wailed in her trust in God nor her pride in truth. But her silence brought even more suspicion in Nobu's poisoned mind.

"You are a disgrace to my court," he spat in disappointment.

'Another rival had fallen. Another victory was scored,' the fox witch smiled.

And now, Nobu's mind would be entirely hers to control.

Chapter 8
War and Sacrifice

Keiko lay beside Nobu, her naked form illuminated by the moonlight, the thin silk of the sheets doing little to conceal the stunning curves that would summon emperors and warlords to kneel before her. She followed the lines of his torso with her fingers, feeling the warmth of his skin, the strength beneath. Golden lights in her eyes glowed like amber flames, lips curving with a sly little smile as she leaned closer, breath much softer than an incantation against his ear:

"Unification, my Lord," she whispered, her words possessed by some power older than the mountains. "Japan is yours… every province, every blade of grass, bowing to your will."

Nobu's eyes darkened as the sleeping beast of ambition within him began to stir.

"What should I do with Hajiro?" he muttered, his fingers wandering down her thighs almost as if by chance.

Keiko pressed against him, her lips gliding along his jawline, each stroke tightening the web of enchantment.

"Send him to war. He will fight for you," she murmured. "Because he wants to prove his loyalty to you."

Then she let that sink into his mind, saying, "And you reward him for his loyalty. After all, he is your sworn brother even though he made a mistake out of drunken foolishness."

Nobu smirked. "I will promise him power and wealth."

Keiko nodded, fingers tightening around his wrist.

"Just keep him away from me." She looked up at her lover with pleading eyes.

The names were never spoken, yet Yuki loomed large in the space between the two soulmates, her presence barely flickering in the dying flames.

Keiko would not allow that torch to be rekindled.

Not while she still had a hold of the warlord.

The Farewell Under the Sakura

The air was filled with the scent of cherry blossom. The delicate petals drifted to the ground in a slow, silent farewell.

Yuki stood under the venerable old tree, her heart racing with every beat and the agonizing weight of the impending separation sitting against her ribs like an iron cage.

Hajiro approached, his armor glimmering in the sun's last light, with that peculiar softness in his expression, which was overshadowed by something darker and unspoken.

Yuki ran to him without stopping for breath, without a single thought.

It was a crash: she was held tight against him as though he could have time in his embrace.

"You are leaving," she whispered involuntarily while her fingers tore at him, clenching the folds of his robes.

Hajiro cupped her face up and wiped the tears from her cheeks with the tips of his thumbs.

"I shall return," he said. "Right here, under this tree."

She searched his face for the truth she wanted to believe but...

There was a shadow that swooped past them.

An omen. A curse.

She cinched him tighter against her, kissing him fiercely, urgently, tasting his warmth before the cold grip of war could wrench him away from her.

Hajiro kissed her back, sliding his hands down the back, drinking in every inch, every curve.

Together, they fell onto the soft bed of cherry blossoms as the world around them faded beneath the burning flame of love in the dying light of the day.

Tracing his fingers down the gentle slope of her shoulder, his lips followed their way.

Yuki felt breathless as her fingers threaded through his hair, and his kisses became fierce and possessive.

As if he were anxious that perhaps this was their last one. He worshipped her body, brushing his fingers over it as if it were covered with silk, whispering her name like a prayer against her skin: Yuki arched into him, giving form, her hands pulling as much as they could closer, more profound until nothing else mattered in all the world but this moment. This love. When the night air chilled their heated skin, Hajiro held her tightly to him, then pressed one last kiss into her hair at her temple. "Wait for me. I will come back to you. I will always find you."

Yuki closed her eyes, resting her forehead against his. "I will."

But as the wind blew away the fallen petals, she felt the ineffective weight of a hand pulling him farther away. And in the long shadows, Keiko smiled.

The Reincarnation of Farm Boy

The battleground was soaked with blood, screams, and smoke. The moans of the dying rang through the air alongside the roars of the victors under the vigorous effort of Hajiro on the battlefield, leading his sword with ragged breath but unbroken spirit.

By his side, Taname was grinning while brushing the blood off his blade against the sleeve of a fallen enemy.

"You fight like a demon, Hajiro."

Chuckling from Hajiro even though his eyes were still on the horizon. "And you fight like a man who has seen war before."

Taname sheathed his sword, rolling his shoulders. "Perhaps I have... in another life. I know I should keep you alive, Hajiro, for something so dear to me...."

There was something that had drawn Taname into Hajiro's world. Right since the hour they met, there loomed an ineffable between them- something as if the cores knew each other long before the bodies had begun.

Taname was loyal, courageous, and strangely familiar to him, as if he had been meant to stand by Hajiro from time immemorial. And restlessness was stirring in him of late.

A Dream of Another Life

That night, while the camp was illuminated under the shivering torch light, Taname lay outstretched, gazing at the stars.

Fast asleep. And there greeted him a dark that was not quite what he expected.

He stood in a vast golden field,

the wind smelling of earth, the warmth of a setting sun feeding into the skin.

And then a voice. Soft. Familiar. "You promised." Taname turned.

A woman stood on the edge of the field dressed in a crimson velvet gown unlike any he had ever seen. Her hair was dark, cascading down her back like a midnight river.

Her eyes...

Gods, her eyes. They held memories he did not remember living.

"And who are you?" he whispered.

The woman smiled- a smile so sad, so knowing. "You know me. You died for me."

He felt a sharp pain through his chest, a deep longing that made him buckle at the knees.

He did know her.

But from where?

Taname reached out. But the moment his fingers brushed against hers-

The dream shattered.

The Unfinished Past

Taname awoke suddenly, heart racing, skin clammy with sweat despite the coolness of the night. Hajiro, beside the fire, queried with one eyebrow raised.

"Another nightmare?"

Taname puffed out air sharply and wiped his palm over his face. "No… not a nightmare". For an instant, he paused. "A memory, I guess".

Hajiro had a brief moment of study before he nodded. "Then let me hear it".

Taname inhaled deeply. "A woman. Strange, yet… familiar. I do not know her, but my soul does. And my heart…" He clenched his fists. "My heart says I should find her. Protect her."

Hajiro took another long moment of silence before he replied. "Then, trust in what your heart says. I have had similar dreams since young. But, I think I found that woman."

Taname laughed mirthlessly. "Easier said than done, my friend."

A grave tone came to Hajiro's face. "No, it is not. The heart knows truths the mind refuses to see".

Taname looked at him then, into the determination of his gaze. Perhaps Hajiro was right. Maybe the past was not as lost as he thought. And perhaps somewhere in this world, she was waiting for him to remember.

Blood colored the sky over the battlefield. Thick black smoke rose toward the heavens, the stench of burning flesh choking the air. Hajiro gripped the sword tighter, the once-glossy armor now stained with blood; some from the enemies he had slain, but most were his own. Taname stood beside Hajiro; the man was gasping for breath. His sword vibrated still with the echoes of a recent slaughter; an ordinary bunch were nothing compared to those beasts. A screech pierced the night; that eerie sound sent an icy coil down his spine.

Zombies, born from dark onmyodo magic.

They had rotting bodies, and now they moved forward with eyes that sported an eerie green fire and then moved all jerkily as well as terrifyingly fast. Kurojin's sorcery turned fallen warriors into mindless beasts-in-arms.

Hajiro gasped out his last breath. "How many more times shall we kill the same men?"

There was a spitting of blood on the ground by Taname. "Until precisely the sorcerer is dead."

A monstrous roar from beyond the darkness burst into the air.

Hajiro's pulse spiked.

Not just zombies.

Something bigger was coming.

A Dragon

The earth trembled.

A searing, uncanny fever gusted through the battlefield, dragging dust and debris into an engulfing storm. And then—

It appeared.

A dragon, iridescent, impossibly fashioned out of shadows and the bones of the dead.

Its eyes were burning sorcerous pits that were tightly focused on Hajiro.

The monster inhaled an ominous voice that shook the air like thunder. Then in an instant—

It breathed death.

The wave of black fire surged forward, twisting and screaming like many souls imprisoned within.

Hajiro could hardly register for the event.

"GET OUT OF THE WAY!"

He and Taname dove aside at the last moment as the flames scorched the earth where they had stood.

This was not a battle.

This was a slaughter. This was hell on earth.

Fighting the Impossible

Hajiro jumped to his feet, sword flashing as he hewed down an approaching zombie.

His thoughts whirled in confusion: the dragon was no beast of flesh and blood; it was some semi-dark creation of Kurojin's will. It would not die by mundane means.

It had been birthed by onmyodo magic. It had to die by magic.

Taname, gasping beside him, shouted, "Do we retreat?!"

Hajiro clenched his fist. "We fight."

Taname smiled in the chaos. "I was hoping you'd say that."

With a roar of war, he charged toward the monster.

The dragon saw him coming.

It reared back, gathering energy for another blast of hellfire-

But Hajiro was quicker.

He landed on the beast's back with a mighty leap, burying his sword into the accursed flesh.

It screamed from the pain, thrashing around to throw him off.

But Hajiro held on.

For Yuki.

For his promise. For his undying love.

For the lost time that Kurojin had taken from them.

With one last earth-shattering howl, Hajiro plunged his sword deep into the dragon's skull through the very dark core that gave it life.

The beast shivered, then became a pile of ashes before its carcass could even touch the ground.

There was silence.

The zombies left began crumbling down as their Master's spell was broken.

Breathless, Hajiro racked his brain.

Taname slapped him on the back. "Just remind me never to be on the other side of an argument with you."

Hajiro managed a tired grin. "Do."

But even as he grinned, deep in the confines of his heart, he felt it.

The war was not over.

And Kurojin's darkness was not yet defeated.

Chapter 9

Awakening of Lord

Evening breezes dimmed the sound of the monastery bell, carrying its soft notes far over the courtyard, where Yuki stood deep under the sacred cherry blossom tree. Blown petals swirled around her like delicate pink snowflakes set against the background of a setting sun.

Her hands were clasped in silent prayer, yet her heart felt heavy. Hajiro... where are you?

For months, she had endured whispers, accusations, and disgrace, all from the wicked schemes of Keiko. Lies had almost destroyed her; faith had redeemed her.

By the mercy of St. Francis, her honor was restored.

Christian missionaries shielded her from the storm of slanders with their unwavering kindness. Their presence in Japan was disputed, yet their faith in Yuki's innocence had sustained her.

There was one danger, however, that the church would not save her from: The desire of young daimyo Nobunaga.

Growing Affection

The footsteps of the great warlord were clear enough,

commanding, coupled with an authority that bent others to the will of his being.

Yuki turned as Nobu stepped into the garden, his unreadable dark eyes focused elsewhere, but he had that something in his gaze that would make her pulse quickly beat.

For months, he had watched her, curiosity turning into admiration. Very different from Keiko, who wielded seduction as if it were a sword, Yuki's virtue, grace, and quiet strength captivated him.

He wanted her.

But Yuki knew that there was dark desire underneath Nobu's rising love.

The desire that she could never return.

"You have been quite hard to see recently, Yuki," said Nobu and quite smoothly halted before her. "Do you fear me?"

Yuki held his gaze, calm but firm. "My Lord, I fear only God."

It was the quirk of an upturn of his lips. "That would be a brave response."

Between them, silence stretched long. The warm breeze brought the scent of incense from the monastery; the flickering lanterns cast a furious, long shadow over the stone paths of the temple.

Then, Nobu stepped closer.

Too close.

Her breath was caught.

"Do not fear me, Yuki, for I have restored to you your honor, cleansed your name, and society knows well your fame," he now rendered softer-if not dangerous tone.

Yuki's gaze dropped. "For this, I am eternally in your debt, my Lord."

A finger would tug a strand of stray hair back from her face, a touch that sent a shiver of unease coursing through her.

"Then why do you resist me?"

A Test of Devotion

Yuki remained motionless, and her heart raced. Time was running out. Nobu was not a man who accepted rejection quickly. She inhaled deeply, steadying her heartbeat.

"My Lord, I am true to God. I cannot renounce this vow in my heart."

His ebony eyes narrowed slightly. "Is that so?" He did not

buy it.

A spark of doubt and frustration flickered across her face. Nobu was a man with war and conquest in his mind. He took what he wanted. But he did not take her. Not yet. Instead, he gave a low, dangerous chuckle.

"Even God cannot keep you from me forever, Yuki."

Yuki held his gaze. "Then let us pray he does."

A long silence fell. Then Nobu laughed hard and deep, filled with admiration and exasperation in equal parts. He had never seen a woman like her. Yet, though Yuki won this battle, she knew the war was far from over. Yuki's Innocence and Nobu's Awakening.

The wind shrieked through the temple grounds, bringing the fragrance of cherry blossoms mingled with a more sinister scent—the hint of onmyōdō sorcery. Keiko stood bathed in moonlight, lips forming a smile that acknowledged the sacred. Shadows danced around her, whispering secrets meant only for her ears. The presence of the Kurojin had crept on her from behind, his inky robes flickering unnaturally, frozen by the eerie stillness around him.

"She cannot live to see Hajiro's return," whispered Keiko with malicious golden flame in her eyes.

"Her light is trouble with the balance," Kurojin nodded. "If she stays, she can sway Nobu against you."

Keiko dug her nails into her palm; she would not allow that.

For too long, Yuki had been a thorn in her side, surviving every trap, every awful whisper, and every false rumor Keiko had spun against her.

This time, Yuki would not survive.

The First Accusation: A Poison

It started with the slightest of undertones. A simple tea ceremony was held within the castle walls. Nobu was set in the company of his trusted men, and Yuki kneeled before him to brew ceremonious tea. Keiko had devised all of it beautifully.

The poison, which was a death that could not be seen, was slipped into the tea before anyone would know it-Yuki never laid a finger on the cup of tea. Then, while the cup was poised at Nobu's lips, a hint of shimmer brushed the water's surface- a divine gesture warning of the impending disaster.

As soon as the taste of tea hit him, his mind went blank. The bitterness was unmistakable.

His fingers gripped the cup, and his keen eyes flicked toward Yuki, who looked bewildered.

"You dare poison me?" He spoke slowly now, his voice low and icy as steel.

Yuki gasped and shook her head. "My Lord, I would never"

But before guards could restrain her, a storm gust penetrated the room and swept out every lantern.

The shadows elongated and jerked, and a figure appeared out of that darkness clad in brilliant white.

Heavenly. An angel.

The truth revealed in the stillness-the poison was poured by Keiko's hand.

Nobu's glance swung toward Keiko, her wrath masked by an innocence she did not feel. But something inside him shifted.

For the first time, he doubted himself.

The Second Accusation: Whispers of Infidelity

Where the poison could not work, it found a more straightforward tool in insinuations.

Castle walls sealed Yuki for her; whispers followed her every step.

"She has been with a foreign priest."

"She is with a child born out of wedlock."

"She intends to subvert the reign of Lord Nobunaga."

Just calculated words to eat away trust, to sow doubt.

Yet, the indefinite power secured Yuki, warding off such manifesting.

Every time she was tested, the divine would expose the truth. An error in the documents. A slip of the tongue by the deceptive servant. An unexpected witness came out in her defense.

Every single time she was accused, she turned out clear.

Because of this, Nobu's doubt of Keiko became increasingly intense every time.

The Spiritual Awakening of Warlord

In silence one night within his chamber, Nobu dreamt. He was in what was possibly a past life, seen by himself, standing before a raging conflagration with Keiko—eyes cold, hands dripping with blood. On turning, there was Yuki. A vision in purest, luminescent white at the temple gates, light enveloping her. Her hand stretched out to him. A disembodied wail rang out in his mind. "You must choose, Nobu. Darkness or light." He woke up in a sweat, heart racing. For the first time, he wondered—was Keiko his destined love? Or was she the poison that made him blind for too long? The seed of doubt, though, was already there. Keiko sensed the change in him, aware of the fading of her power over him.

Dreams, Faith, and Love

From that time forward, the happiness of sleeping at night belonged to him no more. The instant Nobu closed his eyes, the vision found him.

A grand medieval castle, with its spires pointing into the thunderous sky. Far away inside the cold stone walls sat a false king on a golden throne embroidered with velvet, wearing a heavy crown.

Maddox.

A name resounding from the very depths of his being, a name that, incredible though it seemed, he could not confidently claim never to have heard before and yet felt was his for as long as time itself.

Nobu had stood before the very king, a false vision bound with chains unclad in armor. He had power but no honor, no victories, no peace.

And then came the voice.

Calm yet demanding.

"My Child, is this what you want?"

A New Path: The Guidance of St. Francis

Woke in a cold sweat, heart pounding.

That dream haunted him every night now, bringing images of the future with unchecked ambitions, the futility of power when not righteous.

He sought advice.

In the solemn comfort of his private chamber was St. Francis.

The priest, in a simple robe, was a serene presence. Nobu told him everything about his suffering, the visions that tore at him night after night.

St. Francis placed his hand with grace upon his shoulder. "My lord, your spirit wrestles with the truth. You have been granted mercy—an opportunity for your redemption."

Nobu's jaw clenched. "Redemption?"

"To turn away from the darkness and seek the light," St. Francis clarified, "to rule not out of fear, but out of faith."

Nobu had ruled through strength, blood, and sheer force of will. He had thought that unity could only be forged by the sword.

But now, another idea settled in his mind.

What if unity could be forged… by belief?

Winning the Hearts of the Daimyos

In Nobu's mind, Christianism represented a new opportunity for Japan's powerful daimyos to unite and unify—a foreign faith outside of the unordain, a foreign force to calm unrest. Before the grand lords, he kept a steady voice and commanding presence.

"For centuries now, we have fought against one another; our clans are divided, and our lands are soaked with the blood of our people. For how many more generations must perish from this earth before we cease in our madness?"

Some laughed at the inappropriateness of calling it madness, proclaiming, Nobu, "You speak like a monk, not a warlord."

"We do not expect you to be soft, Nobunaga." he said within himself, "I speak as a ruler who desires an everlasting empire, not one that will crumble the moment I fall."

The comments echoed across the chair.

Then came words that none would have reckoned him to say:

"Christianity is not weak. It is an implement sharper than steel and a force stronger than an army. It is the road to authentic unity."

Some listened with interest. Others maintained their skepticism.

Nevertheless, the seed was planted.

As the influence of young lord Nobu increased, whispers of the new era started to fill the air—a time when wars would not be fought but rather those of a single faith.

A Love Beyond Reach

Yet, underneath it all, there burnt a heart for another reason.

Yuki.

He had admired her beauty for a long time, but it wasn't her facial features that haunted him; instead, it was her spirit, her unshaken devotion, the way she carried herself despite all disturbance.

Although there were criticisms against her, she was still evident.

He had been an absolute fool to have taken her doubts and allowed Keiko's whispers to cloud his mind.

And he wanted her now.

So, one evening, with the sun glowing gold over the temple gardens, he searched for her.

Yuki knelt in supplication, delicate hands folded together and lips whispering words he could not hear. She prayed.

He hesitated. His only doubt was that Nobu was uncertain how to approach a lady for the first time.

He finally spoke. "Yuki."

She turned then to him, dark eyes full of quiet wisdom. "My Lord."

He stepped closer, his voice softer than it had ever been. "I have found my path. I have accepted Christianism."

Yuki's lips parted in surprise. "You...?"

"And I wish to stand beside you." His hand reached out, hovering near hers. "Not as your lord, but as your equal. As the man who has come to love you."

The stillness of the air continued for a moment.

Then, Yuki lowered her head. Her voice was soft yet controlled. "I will not serve anyone but God."

Nobu felt his chest tighten. "But I--"

She placed a delicate hand over his. "I am honored, my Lord. But my heart has already been given."

His breath caught. He knew then that her heart belonged to another.

Not to God, but to another man.

It struck like a blade, but he did not lash out.

For the first time, he understood what it was to love someone.

And beneath the fire of the setting sun, it was there that his salvation was complete.

Chapter 10
Crossing Time and Space

Like mad, the wind raced through the vast, empty halls of the shrine, screeching and howling, carrying with it the tossed murmurings of spirits long forgotten. The wooden beams creaked under the weight of eternity, blended with the lasting scent of incense, the memory of cherry blossoms blooming coldly in the night breeze. Outside, the wind was a-tremble, and the trees clawed their branches at the sky as though in defense against an unseen hand drawing closer.

Alone in candlelight, Yuki saw the shadows beyond flicker on the walls. The grainy silk of her kimono spilled over her, the embroidered cranes appearing to lift with her trembling hands. The cold wrapped around her limbs and crept beneath her skin, not freezing her flesh but squeezing the life out of her with an invisible weight pressing on her chest; the aching presence in silence surrounded her in the shrine.

Hajiro had been gone for months in the war. She watched him vanish through the haze of early dawn, with sunlight glimmering on his armor. The promise was still in her heart, an uninterrupted melody: I will return for you. He said it in the very tone of someone who could never falter in that promise, but time had its version; what was once certainty became doubt.

His absence had sunk like lead deep in her bones, an absence that prayers and distant bells could never fill. The nights stretched to a torment for her, nights she reached across for someone who was no longer there, nights her dreams were far more than dreams.

And then she saw them. The shadows surfaced, flickering along the periphery of her consciousness, whispers roaming through her mind like silk kink. Growing stronger, through each night, the visions became vivid indeed, almost tangible.

A castle stood beneath the blood moon, towers pointing towards the heavens like the skeletal fingers of a dying beast. Mist swirled at its base, thick as poison, creeping into the cracks of ancient stone walls. Within its icy reach stood two figures before a towering altar with robes dark as the void.

Two women.

Their faces contorted with malevolence, eyes blazing with an evil enough to hitch Yuki's breath in her throat. The taller of the two tilted her head, a long stream of black hair flowing behind her like ink in water; a torturous smile appeared on her slim lips.

"Matilda," she said, the words falling from her mouth like silk; each word was sharper than the blade's edge. "The lovers must suffer. Their souls will never reunite."

Beside her, the second woman, Cassandra, the sorceress, inclined her head and nodded, her long, graceful fingers moving as if writhing-conjured ancient symbols glowing with a sickly light of plunged magenta. With every glamour drawing life from the arcane strings of the world, the unsuspecting air suddenly became thick and suffocating with the breath of their magic, as one would know if destiny weaved its very threads today against its will.

"A curse that will last through infinity."

Gasping, her eyes snapped open as she bolted upright, breath coming fast and ragged. Darkness pressed in around her from every side, with the vision echo still searing behind her eyes.

And then one unquestionable truth broke in her heart.

Kurojin and Keiko were not merely allies of darkness in this life—they were reincarnations of the souls that had once cursed her and her king centuries ago. Their hatred had transcended the barriers of time, forcing Yuki and Hajiro into an unending cycle of misery.

Her hands quaked as she grasped the pendant around her neck—the pendant that Hajiro had given her the night before he left. The metal, warm against her skin, bore the imprint of his touch and the weight of his words unspoken.

"I will come for you."

These words haunted her, tossed about by the wind and

muffled in silence. But could he? Could he come for her when fate had conspired against them to keep them apart?

No.

She would not accept that.

She would fight.

She would shatter this curse, no matter what.

A fire surged in her chest and evaporated every fallacy and fear that had clung to her. She would be a pawn no longer in this cruel game of fate. If the gods had set themselves solely to see the two torn apart, well, she would stand against them.

For Hajiro.

For the love they bore.

For the promise yet to be fulfilled.

As the winds bellowed through the shrine, taking the voices of the long-dead spirits with them, Yuki rose defiantly. It would be a long night, and the battle still awaited her.

A Secret Buried in the Onmyodo Scrolls

Yuki carried that flame of believability inside her heart, which no water would extinguish. Every night, under the dome of a silvery moon, as the temple bells tolled time, she would find herself deep-seated within the towering walls-within the shelves of the temple archives, fingers rippling on the aged parchment that formed the great scrolls. The warm scent of aged ink and dust encircled her, whispering memories into her ears.

She had read so many texts about rituals, incantations, and spells forgotten in time, spells used once by the great masters of Onmyoji that protected the land from demonic forces. However, none spoke about how to undo this cruel fate promised to her soul and that of Hajiro over several lifetimes.

Up until now.

The candlelight flickered as she finally unfurled an exceptionally ancient scroll, whose edges were frayed and whose ink was barely legible beneath centuries of time's decay. And there-hidden beneath layers of cryptic symbols and forgotten knowledge-she found it.

A passage written and faded, with characters trembling, as if even the ink feared the truth it brought. "Through waters of infinity, that which is lost may be regained. Alas, money must pay for cruelty by time through fate."

Her breath hitched.

This was it.

Tracing the letters of pain thought, her fingers felt the

smoothness of the delicate script, her heart pounding in a mixture of hope and trepidation. The words glimmered under candlelight-touching as if awakening from centuries of slumber.

But there was more.

Pay the price. Sacrifice was demanded.

Her pulse raced as her eyes perused through the following lines, the lines painstakingly clear in their instruction. To shatter the fetters binding her and Hajiro, she would require three holy elements in this life:

Tears of the Moon:

The tear of pure sorrow is drawn from the heart of one who has lost a soulmate.

Bloodroot Blossom:

A flower that blossoms only when watered with the tears of betrayal.

Breath of the Forgotten:

A shard of the soul that is stuck between life and death.

Her hands shook as she was reading.

By now, she had miraculously gathered the first ingredient, the Tears of the Moon. Every night since Hajiro had left, she had wept for him while her sorrow carved itself deep into the recesses of her spirit. Thus, her grief, pure and unbid, had filled the first requirement.

The second and the third remained conundrums.

Bloodroot Blossom: The flower blossoming only in the soil of treachery and nurtured with the anguish of one whose soul was betrayed. Where on earth is she going to find that? Breath of the Forgotten: This is an incomprehensible way of describing some soul hovering between life and death, waiting to be claimed.

Her lips parted as a breath left her lips, for she realized.

For the sake of finding these last pieces, she would cross into another world.

Betrayal and Escape

But she was not alone in her search.

Someone was watching her.

Keiko had been stalking.

She knew every move, whisper, and stolen moment spent poring over the sacred texts.

Then she acted.

On the evening of her greatest betrayal, under the dim glow

of paper lanterns, Keiko's venomous speech slithered through the halls of Oda's court like a serpent through reeds.

"Yuki is a traitor," Keiko would say, her voice dripping with malice and sweetness, smooth and intentional.

"She experiments in forbidden sorcery. She conspires against Lord Nobunaga. I have witnessed it."

The words were lies—poisonous ones. Lies meant to damn.

And the lies spread like fire.

Suspicion glimmered in the court's eyes, and whispers filled the space between the lips curled into accusations. Even Nobu, who once swore to defend her, was faltering. His fingers tightened around the katana's hilt as heavy as with the weight of conspiracy from Keiko.

"Yuki..." he murmured, unmistakable tension in his voice.

She watched—he hesitated, fighting his faith against her and the voices of his advisors demanding a reason.

And, just like that, the final betrayal.

The night would serve them well. The hands grabbed her wrists, vicious and unwavering, and pulled her from her chambers.

She had time for one cry only before she was thrown down in front of the daimyos, her knees bruising on the cold stone courtyard. The flaming torches with long, jagged shadows illuminated the faces of men who had long since judged her guilty.

"Defend yourself!" one spat, his voice heavy with accusation.

Yuki lifted her gaze, her heartbeat steady despite the coiling in her gut.

She could fight. She could plead for her innocence.

Or—she could run.

Her fingers glided toward the pendant hanging on her throat, the last gift from Hajiro warm against her skin. He had promised to come back for her. But she could not afford to wait. Not now.

She closed her eyes and whispered a single spell. The words- ink on ancient parchment- came to life on her tongue, a spell spoken with the power of a thousand pockets full of desperate prayers.

A windstorm rushed through the courtyard. The torches whimpered as they flickered, flames reaching up high as if trying to grasp the sky. Then- an explosion of golden light.

Her bones shattered. Streaks of blurring surroundings filled her vision.

The last thing recorded in her mind as the light swallowed her was the look on Keiko's face, a mixture of surprise and disbelief.

And then silence.

Yuki had opened her eyes to the fact that she would no longer be in Feudal Japan.

The Magical Kingdom of Zuzu and Queen Lydia

She noticed first the light.

She had never seen anything like this silver, soft, impossibly pure light, as though the moon itself had cast an eternal glow on the land. She blinked, trying to regain her vision while adjusting to the sheer, breathtaking impossibility of what was before her.

Zuzu.

She heard it whispered in her mind like an old dream pang.

A kingdom of soft wonder where rivers shimmer with liquid glass flowing in endless winding ribbons reflecting the sky; mighty castles made of crystal shoot up to the heavens with innumerable spires above catching the light and casting prismatic hues throughout the landscape; bridges intertwined in gold arch above sapphire lakes while the very air itself hums with a quiet ancient magic.

But the strangest part?

The people knew her. And as she stood at the heart of impossible beauty, silence descended over the fast-moving kingdom. Then, one by one, they dropped to their knees.

"Queen Lydia has returned." Their voices trembled with reverence, echoing through the streets, the palace halls, and the very bones of the city itself. She stood frozen. Queen Lydia? She wasn't just Yuki; she was Lydia, the lost queen. Something stirred deeply within the buried memory on the edge of awakening. This place, this name, this moment was all painfully familiar in a way she could not yet specify. But before she could make sense of it, she felt it. The curse is tightening. Every moment she spent in Zuzu, the magic that bound her to Feudal Japan, tugged at the edges of her soul as if to say, "Your mission is far from over." She had not come here to rule. It was to break the curse that she had come.

The Quest for the Second and Third Ingredients

The passage of all salvation was in front.

The second ingredient, the Bloodroot Blossom, awaited her at the depths of the Forest of Echoes.

A place where the very flow of time was distorted, and secrets from the bygone past rode over the wind, whispering in voices unknown from this world.

A flower whose crimson petals and sorrow-weaved roots

would bloom only when watered with the tears bred of betrayal was said to exist.

Shivers winged down her spine at the thought.

Could her tears suffice?

Or would greater betrayal have to be faced before the flower bloomed?

Then came the last ingredient.

The Breath of the Forgotten.

An old soul lost somewhere outside time: one that has died but never moved on.

A last breath let out by a ghost.

Her stomach clenched.

Where to find something like that?

She had met spirits before, but since their passing had been so long ago, she doubted any spirit would be willing to part with the final remnants of its existence.

A thought sprang forth.

Should she take it by force?

She curled her fingers into fists.

No.

She would find another way.

But one thing she knew for sure, come what may:

She should never fail.

Because with every ticking second, the curse in Feudal Japan was strengthening, tightening like an iron chain on her soul.

The clock was ticking.

A Love That Transcends Time

A shade above the unfamiliar sky and surrounded by the kingdom she was supposed to rule but could never call her own, one thought remained: Hajiro. The weight on her heart as that name weighed as much as lead.

She pressed a palm to her chest where the pain throbbed, longed, and felt an inescapable tether stretching across lifetimes.

Once, she had lost him. She would not lose him again.

She closed her eyes, uttering a silent vow lost in the silver-touched air:

"I will find my way back to you, no matter the distance or the lifetimes."

But what she did not yet know—

What she could not yet know—

Was that even as she searched for him in one world...

He was searching for her in another.

Chapter 11

The Battle of Souls

The atmosphere outside the physical realm was rent asunder in this grotesque translation of the storm's howl. Jagged streaks of bluish-purple lightning flickered across the sky, momentarily brightening the battlefield below with a savage glare. Gone were the days when the temple grounds of Kyoto stood grand and resplendent, pure and serene, with emotional vibrations. What lay in ruin around the two warriors was a deadly wasteland filled with shattered stones and broken bodies.

Pools of blood mingled with torrential and freezing rain in the mud. The mingling smell of blood and sorcery was pungent, one of charred flesh and decaying corpses mixing with the wind like a ghostly memory. Amidst the massacre stood two men.

Hajiro and Taname.

Breathless and panting, bruised and battered, they stood their ground; of their will, however, some life remains. In that moment of destruction stood a distant figure that walked across the heart of the battlefield.

This figure was shrouded in an aura of surrounding darkness, clothed in midnight-black robes that rippled in the storm wind yet never drenched by the rain that sustained no spirit of life. The very energy of the storm was rejuvenated with fury not against but for him. His ashen face was white as a spell upon the surface and unblemished, except for the tiniest wrinkle of amusement that danced upon his lips.

Kurojin.

The Shadow Sorcerer.

Molten-like eyes glimmering with an unnatural light sliced through the heavy rain as they fixed themselves on the prey. The storm swirled and crackled with energy, sickening and attesting to his presence, wanting his command and in consummate harmony with the Void.

The low velvet chuckle oozed with poison from Kurojin's lips, an unattached doorman for his presence.

A casual "Hah... fools."

A snake's whisper filled the air and crawled towards its victim.

"You dare challenge me, knowing you stand before the god of death itself?"

With a pang of that voice, Hajiro tightened his grip on the katana's life where it hung; all colors flooded from his fingertips, unyielding to pain.

Taname stood close by, fists clotted beside him, although the wounds of crimson stained the tattered edges of his clothing. His breathing stayed even.

No matter how furious the rain fell, they remained resolute.

Hajiro's voice was like the voice of an angry god.

"You are not the god!"

He nullified the thunderous, pallet-saturated rage around him with that very defiance.

"Only a parasite drawing its sustenance from power stolen from the innocent!"

Kurojin laughed profoundly and long, each twitch of the muscle on his face hardening the sarcasm in his mockery, driving the cold wind up in spirals above him and mocking the source of the feeble light.

"Then let me show you how much power this parasite wields."

The flick of his wrist conveyed unfathomable tremors beneath them!

Deep down, an ungodly howl arose from the underworld's pit, rattling the walls of the battlefield on which they fought.

Underneath the surface, the ground cracked open, emitting a musty, thick, oily darkness that pulsated like a living entity. They came from the void.

Monstrous creatures crawled inside that darkness, grotesque things born to disfigure only.

Their limbs stretched all ball joints irreparably disjointed, and the hollowness of their eyes glimmered with malignant hunger. Some scrabbled with clawed forelimbs while their flesh ripped with every movement to drag their dying forms forward. Others slithered like serpents; their mouths gaped wide in devilish grins.

The atmosphere reeked of death and sulfur.

A cacophony of tortured shrieks rang through the air, seeping into the bones of whoever heard it.

Taname tensed; muscles coiled like a snake, ready to strike.

Hajiro raised his bloodied and rain-soaked sword and stared into the horde that grew before him.

He turned back to face Kurojin, still refusing to flinch.

"Then we'll carve our way through them."

Taname nodded curtly, voice low but resolute.

"Side by side."

The creatures surged forward in their endless howling.

The war began.

Monstrous Beasts and the Blurring of Reality

Earth rumbled and broke up from between the edges of the battlefield, jagged fissures erupting from below into an infinity of writhing shadows.

Emerging from the slaughtered faces were unearthly monsters. Horrid, twisted beasts clawed into the world with their decaying flesh and hollow, soulless eyes while their jagged limbs twitched unnaturally toward living flesh.

Serpentine horrors, their bodies slick with blackened decay, slithered among the remains of fallen warriors. Evil fangs dripping with venom hissed and sizzled at the stone, dissolving it as parchment turned to fire.

And above them all, a monstrous figure blotted out the very stars.

A dragon of obsidian scales unfurled its wings, every stroke turning into a storm of ash and embers. Its eyes, however, burned molten gold, reflecting in them the world it sought to destroy. Then it opened its terrible maw, roaring deafeningly:

And out poured a flood of fire.

Flames as bright as the sun sundered the darkness and changed night into day. The air warped under unbearable heat while the earth was seething infernally under it.

But not only the field moved. Reality gained a bend and twist.

Already, time itself had begun to shred: layers peeled apart unevenly in fractures, and memories from the now-starved present spilled into it as if from some accursed kaleidoscope.

Images are fleetingly drawn by shadows dancing in sight. It was too brief a moment for the visions of life.

The Truth of Their Past Lives

The battlefield slowly melted into a golden light.

The war-torn earth, the torched soil by Kurojin's manpower, the fires- all of this dissolved.

Hajiro himself was gasping as his chest tightened as if drawn all the air in it. The sword slipped from his grip and faded from the memory because around him transformed.

He stood there facing the castle. The magnificent structure and the sky-high spires could boast of being decorated in banners of crimson and gold.

And he was not even a warrior anymore.

He was a king.

Clad by royal robes, getting across his chest were threads of red and brilliant gold woven into the most intricate patterns. An obsidian and jade crown rested atop his brow. The importance of a kingdom might have been felt gathering in his shoulders, but at that time, he felt nothing save for the movement of fate.

Because beside him...

Yuki.

Yet, she was not Yuki.

As he knew her now.

She was clothed in flowing silks, in which the emblems of a lost empire were embroidered. Her throat was bedecked with jewels of sapphire and amethyst, and her flowing locks was woven into delicate braids. Moonlight bathed her in silver, a goddess upon the castle's highest tower.

And their fingers were intertwined.

Their love was undeniable because it was woven into the very threads of time.

Then, the shadows moved.

And out of the darkness came two figures.

Sorceress Cassandra. And sister of hers, Matilda. The eyes burned by envy; the faces twisted with an emotion that had long since festered into something rank. Their whispers were venomous, curling into the wind like that of a snake's breath. They cast a curse. Thus, it sealed a fate. Magic rents through the air, laced with malevolence and fury. Stars tremor; castle walls crack; and love sworn to protect turns shattered—repeatedly, through lifetimes and centuries, tied to suffer by soul.

They were doomed to separate.

No matter how many times they are caught between them, no matter how long they've been carrying their love -

Fate would never keep them together. Hajiro bayed. His chest heaved under the load of time lost. Tears brimmed into his eyes.

"Yuki… it was always you..." he murmured.

But his vision shattered.

The battlefield returned in violent rush-smoke, fire, and death. But truth remained. The past carved itself into the deep fabric of his very soul. And fate, cruel and accurate as it always was, would not relent.

The Final Showdown

The world turned, locked into a war's horrid symphony of death and destruction, shadows and fire screaming out of the battlefield.

An unending tide surged as the monstrous army of Kurojin, marching forward like waves made of grotesque creatures, vomited forth by the darkness itself. Their misshapen limbs clawed at the earth, shrieking with the hunger of the damned. Some wear the rotting flesh of the long dead, hollow eyes focused on that which lives, while others slithered on serpent-like bodies with fangs dripping with venom, hissing when they contact the blood-drenched soil.

Above them all was the obsidian dragon.

With scales black as the void, its wings spread, casting over the battlefield an eternal eclipse. Its eyes, burning with molten hatred, marked Hajiro as the last of all the threats against Kurojin's dominion.

Then—

The dragon roared.

Swept from the heavens, shook, and combined with that monstrous sound was shock wave after shock wave hurling over the countryside. Soldiers and beasts alike fell to their knees, clutching their ears as the deafening sound tore through their skulls.

Barely had the time to react when down came the massive paw of the creature, a vicious claw made for rending mountains in two.

But before it could strike—

He braced for the impact, but at the same time—

Taname moved.

A blur of motion, impossibly fast.

"Hajiro, MOVE!"

With all the power of a seasoned warrior, Taname threw himself between Hajiro and the dragon, his blade flashing in the flickering firelight. Steel met scale, the impact unleashing a burst of energy so powerful that the air rippled with the force of the collision.

The ground trembled. Fire and embers danced in the wind.

Taname held the beast at bay, his muscles straining, his sword locked against the dragon's immense talons. Sweat poured down his face, his teeth clenched in defiance.

And then - he shifted his head slightly to meet the gaze of Hajiro. There was no fear in his eyes. Just resolve. "Live," he said, voice steady despite the crushing weight of the beast. "For her." And then -he let go. The dragon's claws were impaled into him. Time froze. The world of Hajiro was shattered. The twisting sound of a scream coming from within his chest gets drowned out by all the surrounding chaos. "TANAME!!!" For a brief moment, Taname's body hung in the air, the balance dangling between life and death. His eyes stayed open, but his strength had left him. Then the dragon threw him away like a damaged doll. His body hit the ground with a sickening thump. Hajiro staggered forward, but his legs felt like lead. Taname was gone. The sacrifice was made.

Taname's Sacrifice and the Fall of Kurojin

A laugh, ugly grin atop the battlefield.

Kurojin stood in a black silhouette against the blazing fires upon the ruin of war. There was amusement cruelly mocking on his visage.

"The waste," he said.

But then—

The air shifted.

A change was coming.

The tremble of the earth began to quake beneath an unseen force pressing upon it once more, returning to its usual stillness.

A golden beam fell from the fallen body of Taname.

It began as soft rays at dawn, breaking through the night, then grew rapidly, burning bright and brighter, until it became a beacon of pure radiance.

Kurojin's expression twisted.

"No..." he whispered.

The dragon screamed, writhing in agony as cracks of golden light pierced his midnight scales. The creatures of the abyss staggered, flickering in their forms as if their very existence were undone.

Taname's final act- his sacrifice born out of love shattered the darkness.

The curse that bound the battlefield was breaking.

Kurojin snarled. His once-triumphant stance wavered as his dark magic faltered.

"NO! IT CANNOT BE!"

Hajiro rose to his feet.

His hand gripped the hilt of his sword tighter than ever.

His rage, sorrow, and love all melded into the final blow.

A battle cry tore from his throat as he rushed forward.

His blade sang through the air, slicing through the remains of shadow that dared stand in his way.

Kurojin barely had time to react before the tip of Hajiro's sword pierced his heart.

For a moment-

There was silence.

Then-

An explosion.

Light and darkness collided in a cataclysmic blast, blindsiding everything in its wake.

Kurojin poured out one final, anguished scream-

And then,

He was no more.

The battle was over.

Hajiro won.

The Hero's Longing

The battlefield lay in ruins.

But now there was silence.

An army of monsters had passed away: their deformed corpses dust in the wind. The night sky, once blackened with evil, had cleared up. Stars blinked into being, distant and serene, their twinkling undisturbed by the chaos that had erupted below.

Yet, with all the victory around him—

Hajiro felt nothing but emptiness.

His feet dragged on, and breath after breath became an effort.

Then he stumbled and fell to his knees in front of Taname's dead body.

His fingers quivered as he reached out but felt nothing; the warmth had already departed.

"Why...?"

The question had slipped barely out of his lips.

Tears started to fall.

One after another, they plopped down on the blood-soaked ground.

Taname had given everything.

For the war.

For Hajiro.

For love.

For something greater than himself.

Hajiro clenched his fists, nails embedding into the flesh of his palm.

He would not let Taname's sacrifice go in vain.

He raised his head, heart pounding.

"Yuki..."

It was the anchor that held him together.

She was waiting for him.

Somewhere.

She stood there past the horizon, past time, and fate itself.

And this time—

Nothing would keep them apart.

Not war.

Not curses.

Not even death.

With an iron will, Hajiro stood up.

The battle had ended.

But not his journey—his fight for love...

That had only just begun.

Would fate finally allow them to be together?

Or was there still an ancient curse standing in their way?

Hajiro could only hope.

But one thing was sure—

He would stop at **nothing** to hold Yuki in his arms again.

Chapter 12

Sacrifice and Redemption

The battlefield trembled under the weight of fate itself. The ground, scorched and littered with the bodies of the fallen, pulsed with dark energy—remnants of Kurojin's foul magic still clinging to the land like a lingering disease. The air was thick with the acrid scent of burnt flesh and the iron tang of blood.

Hajiro staggered forward, his breath ragged, his muscles screaming in protest. His fingers tightened around the hilt of his sword, the once-polished steel now marred with the grime of battle. His body bore the marks of countless clashes—cuts that ran deep, bruises that colored his skin in violent hues of war. But none of it compared to the wound in his heart.

Taname was gone.

His friend, his brother-in-arms, the one who had sworn to fight beside him until the very end—had given his life to weaken Kurojin's grip on the world. Taname had stood against the darkness, his final act of defiance a beacon of hope against the encroaching tide of despair.

And now, as the monstrous overlord loomed before Hajiro, Kurojin's once-unbreakable aura flickering like a dying ember, the opportunity had come.

This was his chance.

But it was not his alone.

Across the shattered remnants of reality, in a realm untouched by mortal hands, Yuki stood as Queen Lydia.

She was no longer just Yuki. The quiet girl, the hesitant warrior—she had become something more. The air around her shimmered with an ethereal glow, her silver robes billowing in an unseen wind. Her crown, forged from light itself, sat upon her brow, and in her grasp, the relic that could end the curse—the Tear of the First Dawn.

It pulsed with warmth, hope, and the cries of those who had suffered for lifetimes under the weight of an ancient fate.

The spirits of past queens whispered to her, their voices a chorus of longing and resolve.

"You are the last child of light. The cycle must end."

Yuki's heart pounded against her ribs, a frantic rhythm of fear and duty intertwined. She had no room for hesitation. She had no right to falter.

Closing her eyes, she raised the Tear high above her head.

The heavens responded.

A pillar of golden radiance erupted from the relic, spiraling into the sky piercing the veil between realms. It cut through the suffocating darkness that had long since swallowed the battlefield, severing the last tendrils of Kurojin's hold on the world.

A scream tore through the air—not of pain but desperation.

Kurojin felt it.

The decay of his dominion. The unraveling of his power.

And Hajiro saw it.

The moment the dark king's stance faltered, the shadows writhing around him recoiling in agony—Hajiro moved.

His feet barely touched the ground as he surged forward, his vision locked onto his target. Every memory, every loss, every sacrifice that had led to this moment burned within him.

Taname's last words rang in his ears.

"Live. For her."

Hajiro's grip on his blade tightened.

He would.

For Yuki. For Taname. For every soul bound by this cursed fate.

Kurojin, once towering and invincible, now staggered backward, his body fracturing, his inhuman form struggling to hold itself together.

"This cannot be…!" Once an unshakable force of dread, his voice now carried the unmistakable edge of fear.

Hajiro did not answer.

There were no words left to say.

Only an ending.

With a cry that tore from the depths of his soul, he swung his sword—

And slashed Kurojin across the heart.

For a moment, there was only silence.

A terrible, aching silence.

Then—

Light.

Lydia's presence had grown stronger.

The connection between them, between time and realms, had deepened, weaving them together in a bond that transcended reality.

"You must not waver, Yuki," Lydia's voice resonated, neither spoken nor heard, but felt deep within.

Yuki clenched her teeth, nodding. She knew what was at stake. She had come too far, sacrificed too much, to falter now.

Before she stood the final altar, ancient and solemn, its stone surface inscribed with symbols long forgotten. The final step of the quest demanded the Tear be placed within its sacred core. With this, the curse would end.

Her fingers tightened around the relic.

This was it.

She lifted her arms, preparing to complete the ritual—

But then, everything changed.

A sharp, violent tug wrenched at her soul, a force not her own ripping through her connection to the world.

No—

Yuki gasped as a great, unseen wall slammed into place, severing the delicate thread between realms. The golden glow around her flickered, dimming. Her fingers twitched, the relic growing heavy in her grasp.

Something—someone—was closing the portal.

And she knew exactly who.

Keiko.

Her breath hitched as her vision blurred, the overwhelming

force of rejection pressing down on her chest like a suffocating weight.

"No, not now—!" she gasped.

But on the other side, across time itself, Keiko's rage consumed everything.

Feudal Japan – The Other Side of Fate

The winds howled like mourning spirits. The sky, once calm, churned with unnatural fury, darkened by Keiko's wrath.

Keiko stood before the portal, her eyes burning with fury, her hands trembling with betrayal.

"She dares?" she seethed.

The portal shimmered before her, an ethereal doorway connecting realms, flickering with Yuki's presence. Lydia's power still bled through, pulsing in resistance.

"She abandoned us," Keiko spat, her voice trembling. "She belongs to them now."

She could still see Yuki's face in her mind—her hesitation, her defiance, the moment she turned away from everything she once cared for.

Once, Yuki was weak.

Once, she was under Keiko's control.

But Yuki escaped to the other land from Keiko's grip.

"She does not deserve to return."

Keiko lifted her arms, her sleeves billowing in the wind as she summoned the ancient power that coursed through her bloodline. The same power that had bound Yuki's fate to this world—and the same power that would now sever it.

"Let her vanish with the ghosts of the past."

Her fingers wove intricate patterns in the air, and the portal flickered violently.

Yuki's voice broke through, distant, desperate—"Keiko, wait!"

But Keiko's heart had hardened.

"You do not belong here anymore, Yuki."

Her hands clenched into fists, and she slammed the portal shut with one final, unforgiving motion.

The connection snapped.

The light extinguished.

And Yuki—was lost.

The Realm Between Life and Death

A scream tore from Yuki's lips as the world around her collapsed.

The altar faded. The air turned ice-cold. The warmth of Lydia's presence flickered, barely a whisper now.

No…

No, no, no!

Yuki stumbled forward, reaching out, but the connection— her only way home—was gone.

Keiko had closed the portal.

Tears burned in Yuki's eyes as she fell to her knees, her fingers digging into the space where the gateway once stood.

She had come so far.

She had fought, suffered, endured.

And now, she was trapped between two worlds.

A sob shuddered through her chest.

"Keiko…" her voice broke. "How dare you…"

But the answer was lost to the void.

And Yuki—Queen Lydia, the child of light—was now nothing more than a forsaken soul, adrift in a realm with no way home.

The silence swallowed her.

And despair crept in.

'Hajiro....' She thought.

Chapter 13

When Sakura Falls

The air shimmered with the first light of dawn as the ancient curse shattered, its fragments dissolving into the ether-like whispers lost to the wind. The Kingdom of Zuzu, once bound by sorrow and silence, breathed again. Long dormant magic surged through the land in golden waves, awakening forgotten wonders. Rivers sparkled with renewed clarity, the sky stretched in endless hues of blue, and the earth pulsed with life.

At the heart of it all stood the Elders' Shrine, where Yuki had completed her quest. The Tear of the First Dawn, now embedded into the sacred altar, pulsed gently, its glow spreading outward in delicate ripples, mending the kingdom's wounds.

From the shrine's steps, Queen Lydia—Yuki's soul intertwined with hers—watched in quiet awe as the land healed. Yet her heart remained heavy.

"It is done," she whispered, a mere breath in the wind. "But at what cost?"

She knew what came next. The curse had been broken here, but fate did not forget those left behind.

Feudal Japan—The Sakura Blooms Again

Far from Zuzu, in a world still caught between shadow and light, the cursed land of Feudal Japan stirred. The Sakura tree, long dead, shuddered beneath the weight of its first blossoms in centuries.

Soft pink petals unfurled, delicate, and trembling, kissed by the gentle wind. Each bloom was a promise—of hope, love, something lost and found again. The people of the village, once accustomed to barren fields and endless grief, paused in silent reverence. Some wept, others whispered prayers.

And Hajiro saw it.

His heart stilled in his chest. The symbol. The long-awaited sign.

"Yuki," he breathed.

His pulse quickened, a desperate hope surging through him. The Sakura had bloomed—it could only mean one thing.

"She has returned to me."

Without hesitation, he ran.

His feet barely touched the ground as he sprinted through the village, his heart hammering against his ribs. The memory of Yuki's face burned in his mind, her laughter echoing in his ears.

The world blurred past him.

He had waited. He had prayed.

And now, fate had answered.

The Deception Beneath the Blossoms

Beneath the Sakura tree, the wind whispered secrets through the branches, scattering petals around the lone figure beneath its bloom.

Yuki.

Or it appeared so.

She stood in a flowing white kimono, her hair cascading in silken waves down her back. A vision of purity, untouched by time. The moonlight bathed her in a soft glow, casting shadows that flickered like dancing spirits.

Hajiro's breath caught in his throat as he saw her.

"Yuki!"

The name left his lips like a prayer, something fragile and desperate.

She turned.

The smile she gave him was soft, knowing.

"Hajiro," she whispered, voice laced with warmth.

He did not question. He did not doubt.

In three strides, he was in her arms. She was real. She was here.

"I knew you'd come back to me," he murmured against her hair, breathing in her scent—wild jasmine, fresh rain, something untamed yet achingly familiar.

She laughed softly, pressing a gentle kiss to his temple. But her eyes gleamed with something darker.

Keiko watched him with amusement beneath the stolen face.

"Foolish man," she thought, her lips curving against his skin. She could feel his heartbeat—so full of love and trust. The same trust that would soon be his undoing.

Keiko had waited for this moment.

Waited for the day, she could take what Yuki had taken from her many hundreds years ago.

"You cannot escape the curse, Yuki," she had whispered when she sealed the portal, rage lacing every word. "And so I will carry out the ancient curse."

Hajiro was a means to an end. A tool.

And tonight, beneath the tree that symbolized hope, she

would entirely turn it into something else.

A Night of Passion, A Love Corrupted

Hajiro pressed his lips against hers, hungry, desperate, a man grasping for salvation.

She melted into him, her fingers tracing the lines of his face, her body pressing against his in soft submission.

"I missed you," he whispered between kisses. "I have longed for you every day."

Keiko—wearing Yuki's face—smiled against his lips.

"Then love me now," she whispered, "and never doubt again."

Under the Sakura's pale glow, they surrendered to the night.

Their hands explored, their bodies entwined, a fever of love and longing that knew no restraint. He whispered Yuki's name as he held her close, every touch filled with reverence, every kiss a promise unbroken.

But she—Keiko—smiled against his skin.

Because she knew.

With every embrace, with every whisper of devotion, she

was breaking him.

This love was tainted. It was twisted.

Hajiro, in his blind devotion, did not see the fox's shadow lurking beneath the human skin.

He did not feel the curse curling into his bones, branding him with an illusion so perfect he would never again know truth from lies.

The Ancient Curse

As dawn approached, Hajiro lay beside her, his fingers lazily tracing patterns against her bare shoulder.

"This is real," he murmured, a sleepy smile on his lips.

Keiko turned to him, brushing stray hair from his face, her gaze unreadable.

"Yes," she whispered. "It is real."

But only for her.

Because when Hajiro wakes the next day, Yuki was gone.

And all that would remain was the ruin of a man who had loved a lie.

The Sakura tree would continue to bloom, its petals drifting like whispers of a love that never was.

And somewhere in the void between realms, Yuki would scream—trapped, helpless, knowing that she had been replaced by the shape-shifting witch.

The night had ended.

And with it, Hajiro's soul was lost.

The First Light of Dawn

A golden hue stretched across the horizon as dawn crept into the land. The once-slumbering world stirred with the faint rustling of leaves, the murmurs of the wind carrying whispers of secrets long buried.

Hajiro lay beneath the ancient Sakura tree, his bare skin brushing against the soft petals scattered upon the ground. A warmth pressed against him—a familiar, delicate form. Yuki.

His breath was steady, his mind still tangled in the remnants of a passion-filled night. He turned slightly, a slow smile forming on his lips.

"Yuki..." he murmured, brushing the hair strands from her face.

But as his fingers traced her cheek, unease gnawed at his heart. Something was wrong.

The scent—it was different.

The warmth—it was foreign.

And then, she opened her eyes.

Not Yuki's deep, oceanic gaze that had once held the weight of eternity.

Golden. Slit. Inhuman.

Hajiro's breath caught in his throat. His heart twisted violently. The weight of a thousand shadows crashed upon him as realization struck.

"No..." his voice barely broke above a whisper.

Not Yuki.

Not his love, Keiko.

The fox-witch smiled softly, her lips curving in triumph.

"Good morning, Hajiro," she purred.

He shot backward, his body recoiling as if he had been burned.

"What have you done?" His voice was hoarse, thick with disbelief.

Keiko tilted her head, the very picture of delicate innocence.

"You came to me," she murmured, sitting up, allowing the silk of her robe to slip slightly, revealing bruises that were not there before. "You whispered my name. You took me over and over. All night long"

Hajiro's stomach churned. Lies. All of it.

"No—" he clenched his fists, shaking his head as he tried to recall the events of the night before. But his mind was clouded, his memories tainted by the illusion she had woven.

The petals on the ground were stained red.

His hands—they reeked of betrayal.

"You took what was never yours, Hajiro."

A cold, sharp voice sliced through the air like steel.

Hajiro froze.

Footsteps. Heavy. Measured. The sound of judgment.

He turned his head—his world collapsing before his very eyes.

There stood Nobu.

His sworn brother. His lord.

And behind him—samurai in full armor, their hands already upon the hilts of their katanas.

Nobu's face was carved from stone, unreadable save for the fire burning within his eyes.

"Brother," Hajiro started, his voice desperate, pleading.

But Nobu did not speak to him.

Instead, his gaze fell upon Keiko—who trembled; her face cast downward, her body draped in feigned weakness.

"Keiko..." Nobu's voice softened though his fury trembled beneath. "Tell me what happened."

Keiko turned her eyes up, brimming with unshed tears.

"My lord. I—I begged him to stop," she whispered, her voice breaking. "But he wouldn't listen... He forced me. He took your woman."

Lies.

Each word was a dagger through Hajiro's chest.

She was playing the victim.

"That's not true!" Hajiro shouted, stepping forward. "She deceived me! She—"

"SILENCE!"

Nobu's roar shook the very air.

Hajiro's lips parted, his breath stolen by the weight of betrayal.

It was over.

No matter what he said or how he pleaded—Nobu had already made up his mind.

"You were my brother," Nobu's voice was quiet now. Deadly. "I trusted you with my life, Hajiro."

His hand gripped the hilt of his katana, knuckles white with rage.

"And yet you dishonored me by taking what is mine."

Hajiro staggered back, a man drowning in the tide of fate.

"Nobu, you must see—she is not what she seems! She tricked me." His voice cracked, his desperation clawing at his throat.

But Nobu's gaze was filled with only one thing.

Murderous intent. Revenge to restore his honor.

"You are no longer my brother."

The words struck deeper than any blade ever could.

Hajiro's body went cold, his soul splintering beneath the weight of his sworn brother's sentence.

And then—the whisper of steel.

The katana unsheathed, the morning sun glinting against its edge.

Hajiro turned his gaze toward Keiko one last time.

There it was—the smirk.

A wicked, knowing curve of her lips.

The fox witch had won.

And he—he had lost everything.

"You planned this," Hajiro whispered, his voice hollow.

Keiko merely lowered her eyes in mock sorrow.

"You always were the easiest, Hajiro."

The air was still.

Hajiro closed his eyes.

The blade sang.

A clean, merciless stroke.

Splashed the warmth of innocent blood.

Then, the silence of death.

His body collapsed beneath the Sakura tree, petals fluttering down to cover his still form.

And Keiko smiled.

For she had not only taken his life—

She had erased two soulmates' bond, once again.

Chapter 14

A River Flows

With the last whisper of Hajiro's dying breath, all light faded from the sky above feudal Japan. His body fell to the emerald ground beyond the Sakura tree, a holy ground once awakened in warm love and now soaked with blood and betrayal. The cherry blossom petals that floated down from the branches above, once heralds of bright future and reincarnation, could now descend like the gloomy sobs of the spirits watching from beyond.

As a tremor did not pass through the earth, so did the universe.

Time stuttered. Spaces dissolved. Yuki felt that in that distant, whimsical land called Zuzu, either through her eyes or via hearing, collapsed. There was a slashing pain in her soul: the very gutting of what was sacred.

The world around her bent. Under her feet, the ground shook, trembling, but not with motion. It trembled with memory—old memory, via her consciousness.

"Lydia?" Yuki cried into the deep, thick silence. The dim light in Lydia's eye flickered like a dying star.

And then—she was gone.

No scream. No gust of wind. No farewell.

Like smoke from a candle very much burned out, Lydia dissolved before Yuki's eyes. All that lingered was a vapid shimmer, as if the world was trying to remember her but may not have succeeded very well.

Then came the crumbling of the kingdom of Zuzu. The palaces turned into sand. The trees bent into themselves. The willow skies painted a gentle lavender sea streaked with gold turned into drab blackness. The falling stars were silent and indifferent.

Yuki was at the epicenter of all this.

Alone.

No more Lydia. No more voices. No more guidance.

Just... dust.

Everything fell apart around her. The flowers turned into ash in her hands. The first star fell to the ground. The rivers became black and bled into the ground. The land forgot its name.

She screamed.

But there was no echo.

No one left to hear.

Stuck between the living and oblivion, Yuki sank to her knees; fists clenched over the remnants of what once was the kingdom made of love, light, and prophecy.

"Why?" she murmured. "Why give me a path only to take it away again?"

Her voice cracked a raw tremor of grief and rage.

Shallow breaths. Her heartbeat dwindled. As it stood, she could not measure sorrow against days long past. She could merely sense hollow voids where pieces of sorrow once resided with a flaring intensity—the crushing weight of pure darkness darkening the sky.

So she did the only thing left to do.

She closed her eyes.

And she went inward.

She reached into the silent core of her being—past her fear, beyond her longing for Hajiro, through the fragments of memories shared with Lydia and her king. She searched for something still alive within her, untouched by the curse of collapsing worlds.

There—

A flicker.

A single flame.

Small but defiant.

A memory.

A promise.

"Love is not lost. It only waits."

And somewhere, across space and time, the petals of the Sakura tree began to fall.

Feudal Japan

In politics, feudal Japan saw the day when Hajiro's head touched the ground, and the heavens grayed in remorse. The clouds halted their wandering. The wind whispered in mourning.

The plum petals began falling.

They floated, hardly above the threshold of thought, from the heavens, not clusters of petals, but individually, each weeping soul sent in mourning. The blossoms wept for seven days without complaint.

They grieved everything beneath their weight.

An imperial castle that could barely be said to have breathed.

The rooftops of the villages, where no one dared speak of life.

Keiko's secret cave, resonating once with the words of the incantations, is now all but buried under the burden of the fallen grieving.

And the pond portal, situated deep within the forests, vanished under the Sakura petals.

Day melds into the night, blurred under the undying rain of petals. No sun, no moon, just snowing petals.

With each passing day, the blossoms grew denser, covering the land until no path remained visible, no structure untouched. The earth had turned toward mourning for the inconsolable blossoming of white and pink.

Changes began on the seventh day.

And the pond, once tranquil and sacred, began to stir. The water quivered as though affected by an unseen force. The surface fissured, not as ice, but as glass.

Paggering fissures resonated outward from the point of impact, allowing rays of light to trickle in, manifesting in a weird silver sheen.

And then, suddenly and without any forewarning-

The pond splintered.

Its very shape crumbled like glass under pressure, fracturing away into a thousand pieces whose sanguine tears were devoured by Mother Earth. The erstwhile sacred pool lay dry, nothing but a current, a river.

A river born of sorrow and flowing with memory.

It spilled forth from the forest's heart, shining like a silver serpent, gathering petals, dusks, and echoes of a world born again.

And from that river came her.

Yuki.

 Not shattered. Not a girl lost in the void of despair.

But transformed instead.

She rose slowly, soaking wet, with petals and ashes tangled in her hair. Once soft with naivete, her eyes now knew the burden of infinite sorrow and the illumination of sacred purpose.

As she stood in the middle of the flowing current, the river spoke to her—distant tongues that could only be heard by the chosen ones.

"You died. You came back. Now rise as the one who remembers everything."

The blossom petals around her formed themselves into a mantle about her shoulders.

And then—Keiko appeared on the other side of the riverbank. Or what was left from the seven days of erosion.

The illusion had started to crack. The skin of her youth blistered away to reveal that beneath was the visage of a foul spirit— the snickering eyes of a fox demon, the aging bones of one led to slaughter by far too much meddling.

She stepped forward, hissing.

"You should not be here," she spat. "You belong to the dust."

Yuki remained still.

"Dust is where you shall be," she spoke evenly, devoid of all kindness.

The river rolled on.

Keiko stretched her hand out, but it melted away. Her legs broke into particles, turning into ash. Her scream was unearthly, piercing enough to sour the will.

"No! I made the offering! I kissed his lips! I absorbed his soul-he was mine!"

But the river had spoken its verdict.

In her wake, the petals would race past her, circling about her figure, solemnly erasing every lie she had ever told. Her scream dulled into gurgles. The body could almost be compared to rotten bark as it shriveled and dusted.

Washed away.

Yuki stood like a statue and watched the disappearance of the last remnants of Keiko in the water. She should have felt satisfaction. Justice. Relief.

But all she felt was a dull ache. The void beside her was where Hajiro had once stood.

Even without her enemies, he would never return.

No portal could reopen. No resurrection could undo the perpetual finality of Nobu's sword. There would be no dream where she could relive that first kiss under the Sakura tree.

She returned to a world where her soulmate was lost.

The tears flowed without hindrance at that moment--not from weakness but acceptance.

The river murmured once more.

"Love comes. Love goes; But a true love will return over and over."

Unsure but slightly comforted, Yuki stepped out of the river, the earth giving away to soak in her footsteps. Her body ached. Her heart bled.

But she moved.

The river followed her everywhere she went like a silver thread on the loom and dash, cutting new paths in the earth to mark the dawn of an era.

Remembering the past, it would bloom brighter than ever.

But not beneath it...

There was nothing.

Nothing but silence.

And petals. Ready to bloom again.

Epilogue
Eternal Blossoms

A soft breath of spring spilled across the land of Japan beneath the skies of the feudal era far and wide. The Sakura tree stood solitary and mournful at a tree-studded hillside, once shimmering with blossoms; now, a stark monument upon which the entire landscape mourned. The wind still revered the soul that stood below—the worthy Yuki.

Dressed in white with delicate blush undertones, her body was almost ethereal in the golden hush of late-afternoon light. Ageless beauty, her lengthy, black hair fell unconfined along the back like a waterfall of ink. The hands were folded gently together, clasping something far too precious to open.

The Sakura tree stood lifeless when she arrived: branches skeletal, and the atmosphere mournful with an aching sense of loss. Time seemed to crawl down over the tree, loading it with grief, but when Yuki tilted her head up to the sky, something old awakened.

An ache glimmered in those eyes—along with every ache from every life she had lived: the battles fought, the love lost, found, and lost again.

She had nothing to say.

She did not need to.

Her wounds alone, her breath, her heartbeat, and the warmth that pulsed down her veins, even in sorrow, were enough.

And the Sakura tree was there to listen.

One blossom, and then another. A tender bloom unfurled from high above her awakened as if by her longing.

A sighing wind brushed, caressing Yuki's cheeks like a lover's.

And then more blossoms fell, and petals came forth like whispered promises out of winter's bone.

She raised her hand just enough to catch a falling petal; it landed on her palm with a gentle touch like a familiar kiss. It is not a smile of joy but one of bittersweetness, a smile only born with an understanding that some love does not die—it simply changes form.

She closed her eyes.

And time fell apart.

In that very instant, the world became apparent, and laughter echoed across the veil of memory.

From the back of the tree, two younger beings of themselves appeared. Yuki was laughing out of control, running barefoot through the grass, with Hajiro tumbling after her in the clumsy passion of first love. He was a student then, topknot barely tied, a boy yet unfurling from the shells of war and pain.

Winds filled with their laughter painted a bright thousand colors as they raced around the tree. Hajiro finally caught her and spun her. She squealed with joy and pressed her forehead against his.

There were no curses, bloodshed, or betrayals, for the hearts were still youthful and the spirits joyful.

There was only joy of love.

The tremor of the hallucination touched slightly like the lake that had caught the moonlight.

Yuki opened her eyes for the second time. The branches overhead swayed, weighed down with vibrant half-blossomed flowers bidding to shower petals upon her feet. The whole hill was aglow with hues of pink and white, as though heaven were profusely blessing her.

A tear dripped from her eye, glimmering like crystal.

"I will find you again, Hajiro, no matter how long it takes," she whispered.

She stretched forth and placed her palm against the tree trunk, anchoring herself into the earth and the moment. The bark felt rough but warm. Under her skin, she could feel a weak pulse, as if the tree were itself recalling.

And there, in the vast nowhere, the soul of Hajiro stirred.

A wind stirred the air, flinging petals around her like a snow flurry.

Love, she would learn, was beyond the comprehension of time and reason. It resonated in her very bones- a song even death cannot quell.

Come what may, in some lifetime or the next, will be him.

And she would recognize him.

By the way he smiled.

By the way he called her name.

By the way her soul recognized his.

By the way the flowers would bloom again.

She lingered alone in the showering embrace of the Sakura petals.

The air was heavy yet still; silence weighed heavily with a million words undone but understood.

Daylight dwindled, and with the last of the waning rays, so did the petals.

Beneath the newly rebirthed Sakura tree, Yuki waited, not in despair.

But trialed with sorrows.

And love engraved in every breath she took.

And she knew her love would bloom again like a Sakura tree, in this life or another.

The End.

About The Author

Liona Karman is a novelist, artist, and a past life-holder. After acquiring her first bachelor's degree in literature in the Far East, Liona continued to explore her visions and dreams as a classically trained artist in America. However, her unusual life experiences as a survivor of date rape and abuse, a near-death experience, and a pandemic loss forced her to focus more on practicing self-love and gaining spiritual maturity and enlightenment. These efforts helped her accept her fate and solve the meaning of her repeated dreams of past lives to find her divine purpose.

Liona's wish is to offer hope, courage, and enlightenment to the lost and hopeless in the world through her sensual romance tales. In these stories, two soulmates are forced to gain courage, wisdom, and enlightenment to fight against an ancient curse. Her multi-cultural background, memories of past lives, near-death experience, educational background in literature and fine art, and passion for history and travel delicately weave this romantasy series, *The Tales of Eternal Soulmates*, with fascinating details, depth, and vivid sensuality.

Author's message:

"Life is not easy, but it is still beautiful!"